THE
PHANTOM
RIDERS

Center Point
Large Print

Also by Leslie Scott and available from
Center Point Large Print:

The Desert Rider

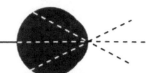

**This Large Print Book carries the
Seal of Approval of N.A.V.H.**

THE PHANTOM RIDERS

Leslie Scott

CENTER POINT LARGE PRINT
THORNDIKE, MAINE

This Center Point Large Print edition is published
in the year 2016 by arrangement with
Golden West Literary Agency.

First US edition: Arcadia House, Inc.

The text of this Large Print edition is unabridged.
In other aspects, this book may vary
from the original edition.
Printed in the United States of America
on permanent paper.
Set in 16-point Times New Roman type.

ISBN: 978-1-68324-215-4 (hardcover)
ISBN: 978-1-68324-219-2 (paperback)

Library of Congress Cataloging-in-Publication Data

Names: Scott, Leslie, 1893–1975, author.
Title: The phantom riders / Leslie Scott.
Description: Center Point Large Print edition. | Thorndike, Maine :
Center Point Large Print, 2016.
Identifiers: LCCN 2016042525| ISBN 9781683242154
    (hardcover : alk. paper) | ISBN 9781683242192 (pbk. : alk. paper)
Subjects: LCSH: Large type books. | GSAFD: Western stories.
Classification: LCC PS3537.C9265 P47 2016 | DDC 813/.52—dc23
LC record available at https://lccn.loc.gov/2016042525

THE
PHANTOM
RIDERS

Chapter 1

The man at the far end of the bar lit a cigarette. The big saloon was poorly lighted and the quick flare of the match outlined a lean hawk face with a rather wide mouth tightly set but with a quirking of the corners that somewhat relieved the grimness of the square chin beneath. In the shadow of a wide-brimmed hat, long gray eyes, black-lashed, glinted coldly. Contrasted to his towering height and great width of shoulder, the little dance-floor girl, clad in white, who clung to his arm seemed tiny as a snowflake and fragile as a flower.

From near the swinging doors, at the opposite end of the room, a grizzled old man glanced along the bar as the match flared up.

"Clate!" he exclaimed sharply, "there's our man now!" He hurried across the room. A tall, broad-shouldered individual whirled about.

"Who—where—" he cried.

But the old man was out of earshot. He detoured around a table, shoved past a group beside a roulette wheel and veered back toward the bar, sidling along the inner wall of the room. A beam of light fell full on his face and glinted back from the badge marked "Sheriff" which winked on his breast. He was directly opposite the black rectangle of an open window.

Suddenly, orange flame, whipped about by blue smoke coils, gushed through the black window square. The sheriff reeled like a falling top, and struck the floor with a sodden, final sound; where his face had been was a ghastly marl of blood and shredded flesh.

The whanging echoes seemed to petrify the crowded room. Men froze in strained, grotesque attitudes, shocked to numbed silence—all except the tall man at the end of the bar. His leap was as the last killing leap of the hunting wolf. In three great strides he was across the room, and in the same rhythmic perfection of motion he hurled his long body sideways and down.

Again flame poured through the window square, and again the lights quivered to the roar of the report. Buckshot hissed through the air, the choked charge crashing the flimsy wall boards close to the ceiling. Through the ragged opening a single far-off star peeped timidly.

To the paralyzed watchers it seemed the tall man really never hit the floor—he merely looped toward it and upward again in a flexing curve. His slim, bronzed hands blurred to the black butts of the heavy guns sagging against his muscular thighs; the room seemed to fairly explode to the rattling thunder of the six-shooters; lead howled through the open window toward the dark alley behind the saloon.

The tall man weaved and ducked as he fired,

presenting a flickering, elusive mark to the unseen drygulcher without. But there was no answering roar from the hidden shotgun. Instead, as the tall man tensed, thumbs hooked over the raised hammers of his guns, there sounded a flickering patter of flying footsteps almost instantly swatched in the black blanket of the dark.

The little dancing girl screamed a warning. The tall man whirled on the balls of his feet like a giant cat, and looked squarely into the black muzzle of a gun.

Things happened so swiftly that no two men in the room ever agreed on the exact facts. There was a clang of metal, the roar of a shot, and the rattle of falling iron spinning across the floor. Against the far wall lay a six-gun, its muzzle still wisping smoke. In the center of the room stood the man who had held it at the instant before— the tall, broad-shouldered man to whom the old sheriff had spoken his last words. Jammed into his midriff was a long barrel still hot from powder burn.

The tall, gray-eyed man spoke, his voice a silky, lazy drawl, but with ragged edges of steel knifing through the silk.

"Feller, you'd better 'splain fast—you haven't got much time!"

The big man tensed at the terrible menace in the soft tones. But nothing of fear showed in his finely chiseled features or his steady black eyes.

"We don't stand for hombres takin' the law in their own hands in this *pueblo*," he said. "I'm the law here, right now, and I'm takin' charge of this sit'ation."

The gray-eyed man regarded him from under level black brows.

"Looks to me like the *law* jest left town," he remarked with bitter significance, flickering a glance at the dead sheriff on the floor.

"I'm dep'ty sheriff of this country," the other replied, "and I'm takin' charge of things." His glance wavered toward the sprawled body. "Pore ol' Hank," he muttered, "if he'd jest moved a mite faster!"

The gray-eyed man spoke again. " 'Pears the *law* doesn't move over fast at any time in this section," he observed. "That drygulching killer out there came pretty nigh onto getting away 'thout even hearing the sound of lead. Even waited to throw a second charge of blue whistlers at anybody who might show a hankering to interfere."

The deputy turned angrily on him. " 'Fore you sound off so big, jest who are you, feller, and where'd you come from?" he demanded.

The gray-eyed man let his level gaze sweep the room before replying. Men were gathered in tense groups, but their attitude was one of numb horror, dread or morbid expectation. Hostility, or partisanship for the deputy, appeared lacking.

With swift, effortless ease the big guns slid back into their sheaths; the slim hands fumbled the "makin's" from a shirt pocket and began manufacturing a brain tablet.

"Slade's the name," drawled the roller of the cigarette, "front handle's got whittled down to Walt. Last from down in the Cochise country."

The deputy opened his lips to speak, but the other interrupted.

"I didn't calc'late to horn in on yore job, Dep'ty," he said quietly. "I just sorta acted instinctive when I saw that hellion scattergun the old man. I'm not on the prod 'gainst the law."

Again the deputy started to speak, and again he was interrupted. A voice spoke over Slade's shoulder, a voice like the fragrance of violets or the scent of roses made audible:

"But *I* am, Clate Shaw, the kind of *law* we have in Cienaga Valley, and I'd take it kind if you'd get the hell out of my *cantina*!"

Walt Slade saw the deputy wince slightly under the impact of that silvery sweet voice, a voice that, for all the music in it, made his flesh crawl. He half turned and stared at the speaker, his unlighted cigarette for the moment forgotten.

The owner of the voice was a short man with an astounding spread of shoulders, a chest like a barrel and the dangling arms of a gorilla. It seemed to Slade that never had he looked upon so hideous a face, for the eyes were of the palest blue, the nose broken and driven inwards, the mouth a wide, reptilian gash in a countenance that was seared and puckered with the scars of old wounds.

There was something atavistic in those colorless, glacial eyes under the black tufts of the craggy brows. So the Dawn Men of prehistoric days must have glared from under the beetling overhang of their low-mouthed caves, Slade thought. The deputy sheriff, Clate Shaw, felt their force, and he took a half step backward. Then his face flushed darkly and his lips writhed away from sharp white teeth.

"Some day, Gordon, you'll go too far," he said in a flat, toneless voice. "You been holdin' yore comb almighty high in this town for quite a spell, but combs can be clipped."

The squat man grinned mirthlessly, but with an appreciative upward tilt to the corners of his huge mouth. His silvery voice, so startlingly contrasting his forbidding appearance, drifted derisively toward the deputy.

"Better aim to keep an eye on the spurs while you're clipping the comb, Shaw." Then the grin vanished and a subtle change roughened the clean edges of the musical voice.

"Call over a couple of your sidekicks and have them carry out what's left of the sheriff," he ordered. "Poor old Hank, he was sort of behind the door when they were handing out brains, but he was a square dealer, anyhow!"

It seemed to Slade that there was an implication in the last remark; but if so, the deputy ignored it. He shot a venomous glance at Slade.

"I'll be keepin' a eye on you, big jigger," he announced, "and you go slow with that gun slingin' here 'bouts. Incidentally, there's a coupla good trails leadin' outa Cienaga."

"Thanks," drawled Slade. "I rode one in. It stops sorta comfort'ble right here."

The deputy started an instant, then turned on his heel and retrieved the gun Slade had knocked from his hand with the barrel of his own long Colt. The squat Gordon chuckled as Clate Shaw slammed the six into its holster with a vicious thrust. Slade was listening to the mutterings of the group gathered around the dead sheriff.

"The Shotgun Riders again!" he heard a man growl. "Gawd, they're gettin' perkier all the time. Cashier of the bank last week, and now the sheriff. Reckon pore ol' Hank talked too much outa turn."

"Don't *you* gab too damn much," a companion grunted in low tones. "You can't never tell what ears is listenin' in this damn devil-valley."

There was silence, and Slade detected a furtive shooting of glances from neighbor to neighbor.

"Shore looks like nobody trusts anybody else,"

he mused. A heavy hand fell on his shoulder and he turned to face the burly Gordon.

"I'm not through with you yet, big fellow!" said the unearthly sweet voice. "Come into my private office."

The words had a slightly sinister ring, but Slade, with a final glance at the old sheriff's body, which was being carried out by four men, followed Gordon through a door behind the end of the bar. Gordon closed the door and motioned to a chair beside a table. He himself sat down at the opposite side of the table, and for a moment the two men regarded one another in silence. Gordon spoke first.

"Well, young fellow," he said, his voice all music, but with a satyr's grin wreathing his thick lips, "Appears to me you've flopped into the soup right up to your neck!"

Slade gazed at him with slightly lowered lids, and at the instant another voice spoke, a harsh, rumbling voice that grated unpleasantly on the ear.

"Okay, gents, stay put with yore hands on the table right like you are."

Gordon started half out of his chair, and sank back, his hands rigid on the table top, quivering in every muscle. Slade made no move, other than the sideways flicker of his long gray eyes.

On the far side of the room was a second door,

leading to the outer air. This door had noiselessly swung ajar on oiled hinges, and through the crack protruded the yawning twin muzzles of a sawed-off shotgun.

Chapter 2

For a crawling moment there was tense silence in the little room. The noises in the saloon beyond the closed door sounded suddenly loud and raucous, but very far away. Then the voice spoke again from out the dark.

"We ain't int'rested in you, Gordon,—yet. You jest set tight and don't make no funny moves. But that big feller is goin' with us. Steady now, this scattergun ain't loaded with gooseberries!"

Soundlessly, the door swung farther open. Two men, masked, with hatbrims drawn low, sidled into the room. The leader held the shotgun clamped against his hip. His companion had empty hands, but the black handles of heavy sixes flared out from his bulky hips.

The first man gestured to Slade with the cocked shotgun.

"Push yore chair back slow," he ordered, "slow and easy, and stand up with yore hands on the table. Then get 'em up slow, and high, and turn 'round and face the wall."

Slade obeyed, without argument. He got to his feet, with apparent awkwardness because of the necessity of keeping both hands on the table, sidled away from his chair and half turned towards the wall, hands raising above his head.

The man with the shotgun gestured his companion.

"Get his hardware," he ordered.

The other started forward, and for a fraction of a second he was almost between the table and the ready shotgun; and in that fraction of a second, Walt Slade acted. He whirled, one foot shot out and hooked under the chair rung. With all the strength of his muscular leg he shot the chair off the floor. It hurtled through the air toward the masked pair, spinning crazily. With a crashing roar, both barrels of the shotgun let go. The buckshot slammed into the heavy oaken seat of the chair, checking its flight in midair as if it had been caught by a giant hand.

Slade went sideways through the smoke whorls, both guns blazing. The shotgun clattered to the floor, its wielder slumped beside it with a choking grunt. The second man had his guns out, but the slugs from them splintered harmlessly into the floor as Slade laced two bullets through his heart and he pitched down beside his companion.

Before the echoes had stopped slamming between the walls, the hubbub in the outer room stilled as if blanketed by a snow slide. For a numbed instant the silence was absolute and void of movement; and in that pregnant instant Keith Gordon acted. He swooped across the room, scooped up the fallen shotgun and thrust it into the table drawer. From the same drawer he plucked a plump sack that clinked musically.

Slamming shut the drawer, he loosened the pucker string of the bag and poured a shower of glittering gold pieces onto the table a split second before a whirl of words and a bubbling of shouts sounded in the saloon. The door burst open and two bartenders, guns in hand, charged into the room. They shot menacing glances at Slade.

"You all right, Boss?" shouted the foremost. "What the hell—"

Keith Gordon's voice knifed through the turmoil like a silvery blade of sound.

"These sidewinders tried to hold me up for the payroll money I had in the drawer; somebody must have talked out of turn and tipped them off. I was counting it when they slipped in the door with their guns out. Slade here downed 'em both 'fore they could line on me."

As the bartender's glance flickered to the bodies on the floor and the gabbling stares of the crowd pushing into the room followed suit, Slade deftly righted the overturned chair and thrust it against the table, so that the buckshot spattered seat was hidden from view.

"Don't know just what yore game is, feller," he muttered, apropos of Gordon's enigmatic act and words, "but I'll string along with you till I get a line on things."

Gordon stepped to the corpses and ripped away the masks, exposing hard, lined faces now distorted in the agony of death swift and sharp. He peered at the twisted features, as did his bartenders and others of the crowd. There was a general shaking of heads.

"Never seed either of 'em afore," growled the first drink juggler. "Did you, Nate?"

His pardner grunted dissent, as did others.

"Hellions from off somewhere," was the consensus of opinion.

"But how in hell did they get in?" demanded the head bartender, "that back door is allus locked."

"It wasn't locked this time," said Gordon. "Somebody must have slipped up."

"I'd swear I locked it myself when I come in this aft'noon," insisted the bartender.

"Then somebody must have unlocked it," Gordon replied with decision. "Funny, though, the key didn't look to be turned when I came in. I always notice that. Reckon they counted on that and turned the bolt back and left the door open a crack. Funny I didn't notice *that*. Shut the damn thing, Slade, and shoot the bolt."

Slade sauntered to the door, gave it a quick glance and pushed it shut. Then he took the chair Gordon had occupied and jammed the back under the door knob, the legs tilted to provide a firm resistance to shoving from the outside.

"You needn't do that," said Gordon, "that's a good strong bolt."

"Mebbe," Slade agreed, "but some enterprising gent musta took a notion to it for a fish-line sinker, or something."

"What?" Keith Gordon swore a sizzling oath and bounded across the room. He jerked the chair out of place and flung open the door. For a moment he started at the empty hole where the bolt should have been.

"Well, I'll be damned," he muttered, shutting the door and jamming the chair back under the knob.

As he came back to the table there was an expression on his scarred face not good to see. He ran baleful, pale eyes over the crowd. They centered on the two bartenders with an ominous glitter. The men shifted uneasily under that bleak stare.

"We didn't have nothin' to do with it, Boss, you know that," one quavered.

"I don't figure you did, or you wouldn't be talking about it right now," Gordon told them with deadly quietness. "But I do figure you to be damn careless and not on the job to let somebody slip in here and take that bolt out. You certain you locked that door this afternoon, Ward?"

"Shore for certain," declared the bartender. "If you'll rec'lect, I came in while you and Mr.

Thorne was checking the payroll money, brought drinks for you both and walked over to the door and looked down the alley to see if Bill here was coming—he was a mite late."

Gordon nodded thoughtfully. "That's right. I'm afraid you were careless, though, and didn't quite shut the door before you shot the bolt."

"Might be," the bartender admitted, but shaking his head dubiously, nevertheless.

Gordon turned on the crowd. "All right, gentlemen, outside, please," he said. "Ward, I'm going down to the sheriff's office before Clate Shaw comes roaring up here. I want to be the first to tell him about this, if possible."

He turned to Slade, hesitated, then addressed him directly.

"Would you mind staying here and keeping an eye on this money?" he asked. "I'd like to have a little talk with you when I come back—like to say something I started to say when we were interrupted. Shut this inner door and lock it, and don't open for anybody but me. Will you?"

"Shore, if you'd like for me to," Slade agreed easily.

He did not miss the startled glances of the two bartenders, directed at him, the heaped gold on the table, and furtively, at the boltless outer door.

"Thanks," Gordon nodded, and went out, shooing the bartenders before him and shutting the door.

Slade turned the key in the lock and walked back to the table, sitting down with a noisy drawing-up of his chair. For several seconds he sat motionless, his keen gaze examining every inch of the windowless walls for possible peep-holes. Satisfied that none existed, he rose noiselessly to his feet and glided to the bodies of the robbers.

With lightning swiftness, his slim, bronzed fingers went through pockets, inside shirts and under belts. Shaking his head, he stood up and stared at the stiffening forms. He had turned out a miscellany of odds-and-ends such as men of the cattle country carry, but nothing by which the sinister pair might be identified, nothing to set them apart from the average roving cowhand.

"The kinda faces you see anywhere on the range or in the border towns," he mused. "Rope marks on the hands show they've been working on a spread plumb recent. Thumb and first finger callouses, but not like what practicing quick-draw men develop. Feller what carried the shotgun is packing a hip holster gun. T'other jigger packed two, but shore wasn't over fast at getting them outa the leather. Why the shotgun? And why was that broken nose Gordon with the angel voice so anxious to get it outa sight 'fore the crowd busted in? Just what have I dropped in on, anyhow?"

"Well, looks like Captain Burt won't see his

little ol' Ranger as soon as he expected. Hafta try and get word to him. Don't know what he might have on hand for me, but one thing is shore for certain—he wouldn't want me to ride out on any such wideloop tangling as this 'pears to be. Gotta get the lowdown on this section, and pronto."

With that Slade sat down and proceeded to deftly roll a cigarette with the slim fingers of his left hand, a pleased expression on his sternly handsome face.

And the truth of the matter was, Walt Slade, whom the peons of the Border villages named *El Halcon*—The Hawk—*was* pleased. The situation promised excitement and danger, and the chance to play a lone hand, pitting his keen brain and his unbelievably fast gun hands against owlhoot forces of evil. Slade did not yet know what it was all about, but a peace officer had been murdered and he himself had been threatened because he had dared fling lead at the hidden drygulcher.

"They work fast," he mused. "I figgered that jigger in the alley had hightailed it plumb outa the deestrict, but instead he musta doubled right back with a pal to drop a loop on me and pay me off for horning inter their game, whatever it is."

He speculated the door from which the bolt had been removed.

"But that was done 'fore they started thinking

'bout me," he declared with conviction. " 'Pears like the Gordon gent was in for a little special 'tention. Wonder why they didn't offer to take him 'long, too? Not hard to figger, though: herding two big jiggers someplace is a good deal of a chore. Reckon they figgered Gordon would stay put and they could 'tend to him later; that shotgun hellion int'mated as much. Wonder who the ol' sheriff meant when he yelped, 'there's our man now?'—and who and what are the 'Shotgun Riders' that feller in the saloon was talking 'bout?"

A knock on the door interrupted his speculations. Keith Gordon's voice demanded admittance. Slade opened the door and Gordon walked in, the deputy sheriff, Clate Shaw at his heels. There was a third man, an elegant, precise little man with keen brown eyes and a half smile on his clean-shaven, clearly featured face.

The deputy cast a glance of scant friendliness at Slade. The little man gazed inquiringly.

"Slade, Mr. Wade Thorne, president of the Cienaga bank," Gordon introduced. "He was at the sheriff's office when I dropped in and came along with us to look these bodies over."

The banker, his smiling expression unchanged, acknowledged the introduction with a nod and met Slade's grip with a slender, firm hand. Then he turned to the dead men and carefully scrutinized their features.

"The men who murdered my cashier, Blackwell, were masked," he remarked in a voice as precise and correct as his person, "but judging from their build, I would say that these were not the men; too short and stocky, both of them."

Clate Shaw mumbled something under his breath and turned to fasten an accusing glare on Slade; but the Hawk spoke first, his voice soft and drawling.

"Sorry, Dep'ty, but I just nacherly didn't have time to send for you fust. I got a notion those gents wouldn't have waited nohow. Hated to be taking the law in my own hands, after what you'd just told me, but the bus'ness end of a gun talks so loud it sorta makes a feller forget."

Clate Shaw flushed under the thinly veiled sarcasm, but appeared at a loss for a fitting answer.

"You show up at the inquest in the mawnin'," he growled. "Reckon you'll be in town," he added meaningly, laying a hand on his gun as he spoke.

"I'll guarantee his presence," broke in Keith Gordon.

Clate Shaw hesitated, plainly of two minds as whether or not to exert his authority and take the Hawk in custody, but unexpectedly the precise voice of the banker supported Gordon.

"I am sure Mr. Slade will be present when the jury sits," he said.

"Okay! Okay!" grumbled Shaw.

He called some orders to men in the saloon. The bodies were carried away and a swamper scrubbed the floor clean of blood stains.

"Let's eat," invited Keith Gordon.

He removed his hat and hung it on a convenient peg, revealing a magnificent mane of crinkly white hair sweeping back from a big dome-shaped forehead. Slade likewise uncovered his head and ran slim fingers through thick hair so black it seemed that a blue shadow lay upon it.

Gordon spoke to a waiter and soon the two men were silently enjoying their food. Finally the saloon keeper pushed back his chair and dragged out a big black pipe which he stuffed with tobacco equally black and forbidding. Slade rolled a cigarette.

Gordon cocked his huge head in an air of listening. Stabbing through the jumble of sound beyond the closed door from the saloon, came an eerie, tremulous wail, faint with distance. A moment later it was repeated, much nearer. The air trembled to a deep mutter that steadily grew until it was an ominous, thundering rumble.

Again came the shrill, metallic screech. The lamp jumped and flickered as a roaring iron monster crashed past the building with a staccato pound of smoke-belching stack, a rhythmic clatter of flashing drive rods and the clang of spinning drivers spurning ringing steel rails.

Followed the swaying creak of springs, the jangle of brake rigging and the click and clatter of trucks over fish plates. The smell of burning coal, of hot oil, of steam and creosoted timber filled the room with tingling whiffs that thrilled and exhilirated.

"Isn't anything like a passing freight train to give you the 'gotta go places' feeling," chuckled Slade.

Keith Gordon frowned in the direction of the fading rumble.

"That's what's back of all the hell raising going on in this section of late," he remarked.

Slade glanced at him inquiringly. "You mean the railroad is bringing in bad characters?" he hazarded.

"Partly," Gordon admitted, "but that's not the worst of it. The railroad, or a branch of it, has just gotten here during the past few months. That's a material train we just heard, headed for the mouth of Cienaga Valley, the railhead just now."

He hesitated, speculated the bronzed face of the man opposite him.

"You know this district, Slade?" he queried.

The Hawk shook his head. "Never hit it before," he admitted. "Never been up in this corner so near the California line. I just rode up from the Cochise country to the southeast, heading nawth into the Panhandle to meet a feller." (He did not see fit to mention at the moment that the "feller" was Captain Burt Morton of the Arizona Rangers, who had just established a new post near the turbulent California border line.)

Gordon nodded as if something was made clear to him. "Reckon when you rode in you saw the mountains just west of here? Well, those mountains are the Palomas, and they're tough and rugged. Those hills are plenty bad; but not a bit worse then the hombres who hang out in them. I was born in this section."

Slade glanced at him in surprise. "You don't talk 'zactly like an Arizonian us'ly does," he remarked.

"Was away from Arizona and the Southwest, nearly forty years," Gordon explained. "Came back here less'n five years ago. Lived over East, in Europe, China, South America, all over. Went to school over East. Had that 'gotta go places' feeling you mentioned as the train went by. Went plenty of places, but got a hankering finally to come back to the home spread.

"Always was interested in the cattle business, even when I was away from it. Found a place for sale here and bought it. Most of it worthless land, but some good acres. Had had some experience in the liquor business and started this *cantina* to help me make a living. Then they struck gold over in the Palomas and helped business. Did you notice anything funny about this town when you rode in?"

Slade nodded. "Most of it new—shacks, false-fronts, clapboard and tar paper. Old 'dobes and stone houses over in this corner."

"Over here is the original Cienaga," Gordon explained. "Named after the valley hundreds of years ago."

"Cienaga means swamp, or marsh, in Spanish, I b'lieve," Slade interpolated.

Gordon nodded. "That's right. Well, the gold strike up in the hills wasn't one of these blazing bonanza affairs. Low grade ore that can be worked as a paying proposition. Worth a lot more with better transportation facilities. A lot of us figured that out, got together and petitioned the C & P to build a line over there. We chipped in to finance the building, mortgaging our profits to get the money."

"I see you got your railroad."

Gordon snorted. "Yes, we've got it—to the mouth of Cienaga Valley, but instead of heading on west into the hills by way of Tonto Pass, the engineers in charge insist on taking the shorter northwest route through Cienaga Valley and over the Black Quag."

"The Black Quag?"

"Yes. I'll tell you about that later, when I show it to you. *It* is going to make trouble a-plenty, or I'm a lot mistaken, but you can't tell those fellows anything. They insist they know their business and don't take kindly to outside interference. If the Big Boss of the road, General Manager Dunn, was here—but he's in Europe right now. Oh, let that pass for the present. What I want to speak about is this: the railroad isn't wanted in this section by certain individuals.

"Over in the Palomas are the hangouts of the most lawless elements of three states and two countries. They know that the coming of the railroad sooner or later means the coming of law and order, and those are things they can very well do without. Owlhoot activities thrive in this district and farther west and south: rustling, highjacking, smuggling of all kinds, including narcotics and Chinese, with an occasional bank or stage robbery to break the monotony."

"Nice country," commented Slade.

"Yes," said Gordon, "and they want to keep it 'nice,' according to their way of looking at it, particularly the Shotgun Riders."

Slade's gray eyes narrowed the merest trifle. "Seems I rec'lect hearing somebody use those words out at the bar right after the sheriff was cashed in," he interpolated. "Just who are the Shotgun Riders?"

Gordon shifted uncomfortably in his chair and his huge mouth tightened until it was like a knife cut across his face.

"That's what a lot of folks would like to know," he replied grimly.

Slade rested his level gaze upon the other's face and waited.

"They first began attracting attention about six months ago," Gordon said. "There was a stage-coach holdup. The driver and a guard were killed, by buckshot charges. Then, during a widelooping down in the valley, two cowboys were murdered. Both had their faces nearly blown off by shotgun fire. Since then there has hardly been a killing in the district traceable to other than shotguns. Once or twice the band, or part of them, have been seen by persons who escaped their attacks. Always they are armed with sawed-off shotguns.

"You saw the killing tonight, and you saw how that fellow who came through the back door was armed. They have the country hereabouts utterly terrorized. Once men learn the Shotgun Riders are on your trail, they fall away from you as if you had smallpox."

Slade's gaze grew thoughtful.

"So that's why you got that shotgun outa sight so fast," he remarked.

Gordon shot him a keen glance. "You're quick on the know," he said, with satisfaction. "Yes, that's why I did it. I didn't want people, my men in particular, to know we had just had a run-in with The Riders, and that you had downed two of them. That would have shut mouths that might do some incautious talking."

"And as the situation stands now, the Shotgun Riders might possibly tip their hand by letting it out that two of their men were killed here t'night."

Gordon shot him another glance. "That's right," he agreed. "The word will have to come from them. That might give a line on them; besides, the thing won't have half the force, coming by word of mouth, as it would if people actually saw with their own eyes that two of the Shotgun Riders had been downed, by you. Which brings me down to the point," he added, leaning forward and tapping the table with a huge forefinger.

"Slade, I'm offering you a job, a better paying job than the usual job of riding. I need men, need them badly, the right kind of men. The way I'm keeping my spread going right now is by selling beef to the construction camp. Near the southern mouth of the valley, the road is building a big yard with shops, roundhouses, offices. They have hundreds of men working on that job, in addition to the regular road builders. Those men have to eat, and they need meat, lots of it. I have a contract to supply the force with meat. It is a short drive and the road is paying market prices. Other spreads up the valley are selling also, what I can't supply."

Slade listened, interestedly, but without comment.

"Getting the dogies together keeps my boys busy," Gordon went on, "but getting them ready for the trail isn't everything. The trail we are forced to use runs through the foothills of the Palomas."

"And you've been losing steers, eh?" Slade put in.

"Eh? I didn't say that!" Gordon probed the Ranger with narrowed eyes.

"Mebbe not, but otherwise, why'd you want to hire a man you don't know anything about except that he's got fast gun hands and shoots straight?" Slade wanted to know.

"Say, you're always about two jumps ahead of me," growled Gordon. "Yes, you are right—I need tough, smart men who can see what's going on around them, and who can act. I have lost two valuable herds, and, what's worse, several good men. My boys are good hands, but they're not gun fighters. They're just hard-working, honest cowhands, and they don't show up so well against those hellions over in the hills. The boys will do a lot better if they have somebody of the right sort to lead them.

"I'm offering you a foreman's job, Slade, at better than usual foreman's wages. But I'm not holding out on you. If you take the job, I figure your life isn't worth much, if those hellions get the better of you. But somehow I have a notion they *won't* get the better of you. That's why I'm taking the chance."

"How do you know I won't wideloop a big herd myself, or go in cahoots with the gang?" Slade asked curiously.

Gordon grinned from ear to ear, an awesome grin that, nevertheless, was not unpleasant to see.

"I gambled a coupla thousand dollars in gold tonight that you were honest," he pointed out. "Wasn't anything to keep you from ambling out of here with that sack in the drawer, not even a bolt on the door. Ward, my head bartender, nearly fainted, when I locked the saloon door and left you in here with the gold. What about the proposi-tion I made you?"

Slade opened his lips to speak; but the saloon keeper never heard the words he spoke. They were drowned by the roar of an explosion, seemingly just outside the door that led to the alley.

With a sweep of his long arm, Slade extin-guished the lamp.

"Keep over to one side!" he snapped in low tones.

A moment later he slipped the chair from under the knob of the boltless door and noiselessly swung it open. Instantly the interior of the room was bathed in lurid light. Less than fifty yards distant, facing an open square between two shacks, was a welter of rolling smoke and spouting flame.

Chapter 3

Standing a little to one side of the flicker of light pouring through the open door, Slade stared at the burning building, which was of a two-story construction. The glow from the flames glinted on the leaves of a big tree standing nearby and smoke rolled through the spreading branches. Slade could hear men shouting, and the pound of running feet. Furniture smashed and clattered as the saloon emptied in record time. Somebody was hammering on the door.

"It's Doc Groves' office—Doc's the coroner—" exclaimed Gordon. "What in the name of—come in!" he bellowed to the man who pounded on the door.

Ward, the head bartender, flung it open. "Wh—what—how—why—" he stuttered.

"Take care of that money in the drawer," Gordon flung at him. "Come on, Slade, let's get over there and see what's happened."

Together they hurried across the alley and between the shacks. They paused under the tree, as near as the heat would allow, and stared at the flames which seemed to fill the whole lower floor of the building. Slade raised his eyes to the glowing upper windows, and as he did so, a face framed in a bristle of white whiskers appeared for an instant, then fell back out of view. In that fleeting glimpse, the Hawk saw that the white hair was stained with blood which poured down the distorted face.

"It's Doc Groves!" bawled a dozen voices. "He's hurt! Get him outa there!"

Instantly men ran toward the burning building, only to be driven back by the intense heat. A short ladder was rushed forward but those who bore it were unable to face the fire and smoke that gushed through the lower windows and wrapped the wooden walls of the building. Others ran around to the far side of the building, returning in a moment, coughing, shaking their singed heads and strangling futile curses.

"He's a goner!" howled somebody. "The stairs has burned through and fell in. The hull inside is all fire!"

Keith Gordon was swearing steadily, his silvery voice suddenly hoarse with emotion.

"Poor old Doc! Poor old Doc!" he muttered over and over. "God, Slade, isn't there anything we can do for him?"

Slade ran his keen glance over the burning building, measured the distance to the upper story window, shook his head despairingly. Through the blistering glass he saw a reddish flicker.

"Fire's working through the floor or up the stairs!" he muttered. "Just a matter of minutes now."

"If this damn tree was just a little nearer the house, a fellow could get out on that long limb which parallels the house and drop onto the roof," groaned Gordon; "but it's too far. Nobody could jump it."

"Not high enough to swing onto the roof, either," Slade said.

Suddenly he whirled and stared up into the tree, noting a stout branch, many feet higher than the one Gordon indicated, a branch that thrust forth not quite at right angles to the other. There were no obstructing branches between the two heights.

Slade turned to Gordon, his gray eyes blazing with excitement.

"A rope," he exclaimed, "a rope in a hurry! Where can we get one?"

"There's a hitchrack fronting the saloon; there's sure to be horses there, with their rigs on," replied Gordon.

"Come on!" the Hawk barked. "Show the way!"

Together they skirted the saloon building, at a dead run. Gordon was right. At the hitchrack were a number of snorting horses, greatly excited by the flickering glow and the crackle of the flames they could not see. At the saddles of several hung lariats.

To unloop one was the work of a moment. Back to the scene of the fire raced the Hawk and Gordon. Looping the rope over his shoulder, Slade swarmed up the tree. It was a hard climb, for there were few branches and the hole was large; but clinging with fingers, arms and feet, he made it to the high branch which thrust out toward the roof.

Crawling out as far as the strength of the limb would permit, he tied the rope securely to its steady support. Then he worked back to the trunk and slid down the tree again until his feet rested upon the lower branch, which paralleled the burning building. In his hand he held the lower length of the strong rope, which sloped upward at a fairly wide angle.

Carefully he measured the distance to the glowing second story window, behind which the flames now leaped and flickered.

"If I could just swing straight toward it, it would be easy," he muttered; "but I'll be swinging at an angle, and if I don't let go at just the right minutes, I'll hit the side of the house and fall into the fire."

Grimly he gripped the rope with sinewy hands.

"You'll kill yourself, you damn fool!" howled Keith Gordon from below, as it dawned upon him what the Hawk intended attempting.

Other voices shouted protests. Slade however, made no reply. He fully realized the chance he was taking. If he crashed into the wall the shock would doubtless stun him and he would drop into the inferno at the base of the building, with no hope of rescue. Once again he measured the distance with a steady eye, gathered himself together and leaped outward.

With a swishing rush he swung toward the building. The hot breath of the fire struck him like a blow. His eyes were dazzled, his senses numbed. Slanting before him for a fleeting instant was the red glow of the second story window. Another fleeting instant and he would be past. But in that granted flicker of time, he let go the rope.

For a terrible moment he thought he had miscalculated. Then he struck the window with a prodigious clang-jangle of smashing glass and a grind of splintering wood. His body hurtled through the ragged opening, hit the window frame with a stunning force and dropped to the floor inside the room. His senses whirled from the impact and he lay helpless to raise himself from the floor, which was almost too hot to touch. All around were flickering flames, and from the open mouth of the stairway roared a blistering column of fire.

Still Walt Slade lay helpless, trying to force his paralyzed muscles to obey the clamorings of his brain. The heat sapped his strength, the smoke stifled him. The despairing shouts of those outside the building seemed far, far away. Desperately he tried to rise, and fell back gasping.

A sudden pain stabbed his left arm, a searing

biting pain, that quivered his nerves, sent the blood coursing madly through his veins and set his heart to pounding. He writhed away from it, gasping and panting. Another agonizing stab and his numbed muscles awoke to frenzied action. He rolled over, put his hand on a glowing ember and floundered back in a convulsion that brought him to his knees.

Choking and coughing, he shook his whirling head and with a final mighty effort got to his feet. A blast of comparatively cool air, pouring through the shattered window, swept the final cobwebs from his mind. His brain cleared and he glared about with stinging eyes.

Almost at his feet lay the flaccid body of the old doctor. Stooping, he gathered it in his arms and staggered to the window, the fire blistering his back, his clothes smoking with the heat. A wild yell greeted his appearance, and a chorus of useless advice.

"Gordon!" he called hoarsely. "Keith Gordon!"

"Here I am," came back the silvery peal of the saloon keeper's voice. "What do you want me to do?"

"Get the rope!" croaked the Hawk. "Tie a rock to the end and throw it through the window. Hurry—can't stand much more of this."

Followed an eternity of scrambling for a suitable stone, and another eternity of fumbling the rope about it and tieing hard and fast.

"Stand clear!" yelled Gordon, "here she comes!"

Slade stood to one side, and an instant later the stone thudded on the burning floor. Slade grasped the dangling rope and drew in the slack. For an instant he stood on the window sill, clasping the old doctor's unconscious form to his breast with one sinewy arm. With the other hand he gripped the rope, taking a single turn about his wrist. Then he leaped outward with all his strength. The rope was all but torn from his grasp as he swung away from the burning building.

Far out toward the tree trunk he swung, letting the line slip through his scorched fingers. It was a white agony of flame whipping about his wrist, but he dared not let it slip too fast. As it was, he struck the ground with prodigious force, was knocked off his feet and sent rolling, gasping for breath, his brain whirling with the shock.

As best he could he protected the body of the old man, taking the brunt of the fall on his own broad shoulders. In his ears sounded wild yells, and a moment later hands were removing his unconscious burden and helping him to his feet.

In a daze he heard the exultant voice of Keith Gordon and the precise, congratulating accents that he recognized as belonging to Wade Thorne, the banker. Rubbing his aching head with one blistered hand, he grinned down at them from his great height.

"If hell's any hotter, I don't wanta go there," he

replied in answer to the anxious questions flung at him. "Otherwise, I reckon I'm okay. How's the old man?"

"Thanks to you, he will live," said the precise Thorne.

"Uh-huh, he's okay—already beginnin' to swear," grumbled another voice.

Slade glanced at the speaker and recognized the handsome, sullen features of the deputy sheriff, Clate Shaw. The deputy did not look friendly, but wore an expression of grudging admiration, nevertheless.

"You're a big skookum he-man, no matter what else you are, feller," he growled, and turned again to the old doctor, who was sitting up, cursing with amazing fluency.

"How the hell do I know what happened?" Groves bawled in answer to Shaw's question. "I was in bed when all hell busted loose downstairs. Knocked me clean outa the bed. I jumped up, fell down and hit my haid 'gainst a table leg or somethin.' When I come to the hull place was a-fire. Tried to crawl to the stairs, but the heat druv me back. Last I rec'lect is clawin' up toward the window. How'd I get out?"

They told him, enthusiastically.

"Help me up, some of you horned toads!" cried Groves. "I want to shake hands with that feller."

"And now you'd better come over to my place

and get your head plastered up," suggested Keith Gordon. "You won't be able to hold the inquest in the morning."

Doc Groves swore an oath hotter than the blazing building.

"Inquest, hell!" he concluded. "There ain't gonna be any inquest. You hafta have bodies to hold an inquest!"

Walt Slade's glance centered on the old coroner's face for an instant. Then he glanced with narrowed eyes at the seething welter of flames that had been the coroner's office.

"Meaning the bodies are in there?" he asked quietly.

"All three of them," Doc Groves grunted, swabbing at his bloody face with the tail of his nightshirt. "Pore ol' Hank's, and them two robbers Clate and Mr. Thorne brung in."

For a long moment, Slade stared at the burning building, his lips a hard line, but he offered no comment.

Chapter 4

Doc Groves was at a loss as to the precise origin of the fire which destroyed his office, but he hazarded a guess while discussing the matter in Gordon's saloon with Slade, Wade Thorne, the deputy and others.

"I had a drum of oil for my lamps and heater in the back room," said Doc. "Mebbe a spark got to that somehow and she blew up. *Somethin'* shore blew up, the way the fire got scattered all around right from the start. The hull downstairs was a-fire by the time I got my senses back after bein' blowed outa bed."

"There was an explosion, all right; we all heard it," Keith Gordon corroborated.

"It must o' been that oil," Doc declared. "Stray spark from a pipe or a cigarette, I reckon. Blowed in the window, mebbe. Never knew heating oil to act like that before. Musta have been a leak in the drum."

This was generally accepted by those present as the explanation. Walt Slade made no comment. He asked what appeared to be an irrelevant question.

"Where were the bodies of the dead men?"

"In the back room," Doc replied. "I had 'em laid out there all ready for the coroner's jury t'morrer."

Slade left the saloon soon afterward. Keith Gordon followed him to the outer door.

"Well?" he queried, "what about it? Going to take that job?"

"I'll take it," Slade replied quietly. "When do I start?"

"Be here in the morning," Gordon replied. "We'll ride out to the ranch together and I'll introduce the boys and give you the general lay of the land."

Slade nodded agreement, and headed for bed. First, however, he assured himself that Shadow, his big black horse was properly cared for and comfortable for the night.

"Looks like we're sorta in for a time, feller," he told the black horse as the velvety black muzzle nuzzled his hand.

Shadow snorted cheerfully and appeared to look pleased. Slade tweaked a forward-pricked ear and Shadow bared white teeth and apparently endeavoured to "chaw off" his owner's arm. With a final pat, Slade repaired to the little room above the stalls, which he had rented for the night.

Like many men who ride much alone, Slade had formed the habit of talking to his horse, and even, at times to his guns. Now as he carefully cleaned and oiled the big long-barrelled sixes, he conversed familiarly with them and discussed the evening's happenings. The ominous metallic clicks of the deadly mechanism seemed to interpolate terse answers and laconic comments.

"'Pears to be a plumb nice section hereabouts," he declared cheerfully. "Folks on the prod generally. A new railroad always brings plenty of trouble with it, and this one 'pears to be a little better'n average. Those Paloma Mountains look salty and the kinda country salty hombres hole up in. California line close, making it easy for shifty gents to slide across when sheriffs on this side get too nosey.

"Same thing stands for gents of like calibre on the other side the line. Then it's a straight shoot down to Mexico, and not so over far, either, when real rope trailing is in order. Good going up inter Utah, too, and I wouldn't be surprised if quite a few dogies from the big spreads up in that direction get shoved down this way. Mighty few inspectors along the Mexican Border over here, and a good market for blotted cattle."

He paused to squint along a black barrel and to slip deadly looking cartridges into the cylinder of the Colt. He sniffed the pungent tang of oil and burned powder which clung to the gun, and drew a deep breath.

"But the railroad will change all that, in time, and in comparatively short time, too. The Paloma owlhoots know that, and it isn't any wonder they're het up. Reckon they'll do all they can to halt the road this side the hills. Things like that have been done before and roads held up for years. Some even abandoned. These spurs inter good mining and cattle country are different from the big cross-country lines.

"The building is often financed by the property owners in the section, as it 'pears this one is. Sometimes they can be stopped, or turned aside. Well, that hadn't oughta be 'lowed. Railroads mean prosperity and progress for a section, with decent folks coming in to build homes and settle, and that's good for Arizona and the whole country. Reckon those Shotgun Riders are some gents who'd like to keep things as they are. We'll see 'bout that. Anyhow, it seems they done in the sheriff, and that's outa order, too."

He thrust a cleaned and loaded gun into its carefully oiled and worked-out holster and addressed the other as he filled the cylinder.

" 'Pears they, or somebody, shore didn't want those two bodies to lay there to be looked over by all and sundry. Looks like they mighta been scairt somebody would see something they didn't want seen. Anyhow, that fire didn't start from a cigarette or a stray spark. A drum of heating oil doesn't blow up that way.

"Somebody set a fire, with a nice charge of blasting powder planted to blow the oil drum to smithereens and scatter the fire all over the room so's it couldn't be put out and so the bodies couldn't be gotten out. Who? Well, that's sorta hard to say at this stage of the game, but my 'sperience has been that folks who talk good aren't allus as good as they talk."

The second gun slid into its sheath and Walt Slade stood up, stretching his long arms above his head. On his lean, hawk-face was an expression of pleased anticipation.

And the expression was not misleading. With the promise of action, excitement and deadly danger in the offing, the Hawk *was* pleased.

Ten minutes later he was sound asleep, his breathing deep and regular, and practically inaudible, his black head resting on one corded forearm. It was the kind of sleep enjoyed by a basking mountain lion or a wolf pausing a moment from the hunt—restful, satisfying, but keyed to instantly snap into alert wakefulness.

Outside the noises of the turbulent cattle and mining town ebbed to comparative silence. The crowds at the bars were thinning out. Men stumbled forth into the clear air to seek sodden sleep. Dance floor girls, weary, heavy-eyed, their senses dulled by hours of uproar and discordancies that masqueraded as music, vanished one by one through side doors. Grumpy bartenders frowned at die-hard drinkers. The waxen faced dealers at the poker tables shuffled the cards in mechanical fashion. The roulette wheels seemed to creak and the skipping balls acquired a querulous note.

Night brooded darkly over mountain and desert and prairie, the stars golden against purple-black velvet, the towering peaks of the Palomas rimmed about with palest silver of reflected star sheen. A material train thundered westward, swathed in a staccato rhythm of hammered steel, rumbled into a dimming blanket of shambling echoes and ceased to be save for a memory-tang of sulphurous smoke and scorching oil. Cienaga slept, or seemed to.

Walt Slade was shot from his slumber by a horrible, wrathful scream followed instantly by a crash and a frightful shriek of agony and terror. As he swung his feet to the floor, reaching instinctively for his guns, there sounded a rattling clatter on the stairs without, another shriek and a dreadful worrying sound—thrashing and stamping threaded through with savage, snuffling snorts.

Shoeless, shirtless, a gun in either hand, Slade rushed to the door and flung it open. As he did so, long lances of flame gushed up the stairs. Lead stormed through the air and thudded sullenly into the roof boards. Then the stable door banged open and shut. Slade bounded down the stairs, crashed into a huge body and bounced back. Another vicious scream knifed the quivering air.

"Hold it, Shadow, hold it!" the Hawk called. A wrathful snort answered him, then an explaining whinney. The terrible stamping and gnashing ceased.

49

In the back of the stable sounded a thumping and thrashing about, and a bellow of profanity. There was a gleam of light and the old stable keeper barged from his sleeping-room, a flickering lamp in one hand, a huge revolver in the other.

"What the blankety-blank-blank is goin' on here?" he bawled.

"Easy, feller," Slade told him. "I don't know what all has happened, but it isn't nice. Bring that light over this way."

Snorting and grunting, the keeper obeyed. He held the lamp high, peering suspiciously. The light rays fell on a tall head with rolling red eyes and white teeth bared. Those white teeth were blotched and splashed with horrible stains, and as the stableman's glance dropped to what lay at the black horse's feet, he gulped and gasped.

Slade's own throat felt tight, his mouth dry. With narrowed eyes he stared at the awful thing that once had been a man—a torn, broken and battered thing mired in blood.

"I was afraid we'd find something like that when I heard Shadow scream," he said a trifle thickly.

"My Gawd, what made him do it? What happened?" quavered the stable keeper.

He shambled forward a pace, stooping and peering.

"Look out!" Slade warned suddenly. "What's that by yore foot?"

The stableman sidestepped frantically, and almost dropped the lamp. Then he stooped and picked up the object, holding it gingerly at arm's length and as far away from the lamp flame as possible.

"Three gi'nt powder cartridges, capped and fused!" he gurgled. "Now what in the devil."

Slade's sudden exclamation interrupted him. The Arizona Ranger pointed to a bleeding gash on Shadow's glossy haunch.

"Not deep—didn't do more than grain the skin," he muttered. "*That's* what set him off!" He gestured to the battered body on the stable floor.

"Was two of them," he exclaimed quickly. "One was sneaking up the stairs, evidently. I reckon he had that bundle of dynamite. The other waited down here, I figger. Somehow, he musta bumped inter Shadow. The rear of his stall is right by the stairway. I reckon it gave the jigger an awful start and he lashed out with a knife— see there's the knife on the floor over there."

"The sting of the steel was enough for Shadow. He busted his halter, whirled about and went to work on that hellion. Mebbe kicked blazes out of him fust. Anyhow, he did him up proper before I could get down the stairs and learn what was going on. The other jigger heard the row and hightailed. Musta dropped his dynamite as he went out. Stopped to throw lead at me when he heard my door open.

"If I'd barged out fust thing, he'd have drilled me dead center. He streaked through the stable door soon as he had pulled trigger. I knew Shadow was maverickin' 'round down here someplace and was scairt to take a chance on shooting."

"But what's it all about?" demanded the stable-keeper. "What's two hellions snukin' in here with a bundle of dynamite for? What'd they want?"

Slade glanced at the dead man before replying.

"Reckon they sorta didn't like me, for some reason or other," he said quietly. "I had a run-in with a coupla jiggers up to Keith Gordon's *cantina*. I've a notion these two were friends of theirs. If they'd managed to set off that dynamite outside my door, they would have shore evened the count—wouldn't been a piece of me big 'nough for a decent burying!"

In a few terse sentences he recounted the happenings in the saloon.

"Sorry I brought a racket to yore place," he concluded. "Reckon I'd better move out 'fore something else busts loose."

The old stablekeeper swore an appalling oath. "Like blankety-blank-blank you're movin' out!" he stormed. "You paid for yore room and yore horse's keep didn't yuh? When Bart Coster makes a bargain he sticks by it, come hell or high water. They ain't no snukin', drygulchin' hyderphobia skunks gonna run a customer outa my place so long as I got the gumption to wag this hawglaig. You get the hell back to bed and forget all 'bout this. I'll lock the doors and keep a eye on things till daylight. Say, that's a real hoss yuh got there. I like a hoss with guts, ready to fight for hisself and his boss."

He reached forth a fearless hand and stroked the black's glossy neck. Shadow responded with a soft whinney and thrust his nose into the seamed old palm. Bart Coster tweaked his upper lip and swore affectionately.

Slade, meanwhile, was examining the mangled body of the dead man. The great black had done his work well and it seemed to the Hawk that there wasn't a whole bone left in the man's body. The distorted face was swarthy, high of cheek-bone, prominent as to nose, with a thin gash of a mouth, now writhen back from nicked yellow teeth.

"Half-breed Yaqui, I'd say," the Hawk muttered. "Mebbe some Apache blood, can't say for shore."

He sniffed at the unusual odor which seemed to cling to the dead man's clothes. Old Bart Coster also noticed it.

"Smells like he'd spilled kerosene oil on his-self," grunted the oldster, wrinkling his nose. "Reckon the hellion had been stealin' a ride on the railroad."

Slade nodded but offered no comment. He went through the dead man's pockets, turning out a miscellany of odds and ends, but nothing of significance, until he came to a shirt pocket with a buttoned-down flap. From this he drew forth three loaded shotgun cartridges.

Old Bart was looking the other way at the moment and Slade quickly slipped the big shells into his own pocket. A moment later he stood up, dusting off his hands.

"Nothing on him to say who he is or where he come from," he remarked. "Reckon the sheriff and coroner had better be notified."

"I'll 'tend to it in the mawnin'," grunted Coster. "No sense in wakin' them fellers up this time o'night."

Slade nodded. Then he fixed old Bart with his steady gaze.

"Do me a favor, oldtimer?" he asked softly.

"Shore," Coster grunted readily. "What is it?"

"When you tell the sheriff 'bout this jigger, don't mention anything 'bout those dynamite cartridges they figgered to set off outside my door," Slade replied. "Just make out this jigger was cashed in while trying to lift a horse from the stable."

Old Bart stared a moment, then shrugged his scrawny shoulders.

"Okay by me," he agreed. "Reckon you got yore reasons for not wantin' it knowed them hellions was out to git you. Well, that's yore business, so far as I'm concerned. Anyhow, I sized yuh up fust off as a bit of all right—yuh're shore sizeable 'nough, anyhow—" with a glance at the Ranger's towering form and wide shoulders— "and I allus trust a feller that a hoss 'pears to think a mighty lot of. Now you git the hell to bed and leave things to me. See yuh come mawnin.' "

Before going back to sleep, Slade sat on the edge of his bed and thoughtfully rolled a cigarette. On a nearby table rested the dynamite cartridges, from which he had carefully removed the cap and fuse. Beside them lay the shotgun shells. He eyed them in a speculative manner.

"Shotgun Riders again, eh?" he mused. "Persistent cusses, all right. Well, 'tween Shadow and me, we've 'counted for three of them. That's a pretty good start—not at all bad for one night."

He smiled with satisfaction as he stretched out on his couch. But perhaps even the Hawk would not have smiled could he have seen the grim band which at that very moment rode out of town, headed north by west toward the dark mouth of Cienaga Valley.

At their head rode a tall, broad-shouldered man with a neckerchief muffled high about the lower portion of his face, so that little could be seen of his features save the glint of hard eyes in the shadow of his long-drawn hatbrim. Across his saddle bow wrested a sawed-off shotgun. His followers were similarly armed. Very purposefully they rode, the rearmost leading three saddled and bridled, but riderless, horses.

Chapter 5

Slade was awakened by a rumble of voices in the stable below. He dressed quickly and went downstairs. The stable was full of men, including Clate Shaw and Doc Groves, the coroner, his hoary head swathed in bandages but with a truculent gleam in his faded blue eyes. Doc greeted the Ranger warmly, but the deputy glowered.

"You're shore mowin' a swath, feller," Shaw grumbled. "Two for you and one for yore hoss. If you keep up at this rate you'll thin out the population till we won't need a census."

"They deserve a medal, both of 'em!" Doc Groves declared. "I'm settin' on this hellion right now. Line up over there, you fellers I swore in, and let's get this over with."

The inquest was short, the verdict of the coroner's jury terse and pithy. Stripped of legal phraseology it amounted to, "The damn wide-looper had it comin' and the hoss has a vote of thanks comin' from the community."

An hour later Slade and Keith Gordon rode out of town, heading for the latter's Slash K ranch in Cienaga Valley. Paralleling the trail for several miles was the right-of-way of the C & P railroad, the twin ribbons of steel gleaming in the early sunshine and fading away into the distance until the rails seemed to merge into one. The hour was early, the sun still low in the heavens. The grass heads glowed with purple dew-fire and there was an autumn sharpness in the air. Slade breathed deeply and his green eyes glowed.

"Mighty nice looking country," he commented.

"Wait until you see Cienaga Valley," retorted Gordon; "and the prettiest appearing stretch is up at this end—so green and lush and level. Sure is deceiving. Up here is the Black Quag."

"I rec'lect you mentioning something about the Black Quag last night," Slade reminded expectantly.

Gordon, however, merely shrugged, and repeated his promise of the night before.

"Tell you about it when you see it. Ten miles to go yet before we reach the construction camp and the mouth of the valley."

They rode in silence for some time, Gordon apparently occupied with his own thoughts, which, judging from his frowning brows and the set of his huge mouth, were not wholly pleasant.

Slade busied himself with studying the country. He turned in his saddle and glanced back the way they had come. A curl of smoke marked the site of the town of Cienaga, hidden now by a shoulder of hills. Farther to the southeast gleamed the wide expanse of desert country across which Slade had ridden in the course of his journey northward from the Cochise country.

Due east, beyond a tongue of rolling rangeland, an arm of the desert stretched northward farther than the eye could reach. To the west were the frowning battlements, the broken crags and sky-raking spires of the Palomas.

They were riding over broken ground now, with a jumble of low hills, flanking the trail on either side. The railroad had edged farther to the west, where an easier grade was obtainable, and the ribbons of steel were no longer to be seen. A growling mutter that swiftly grew to a rumbling roar, flattened and furred by distance, told of a passing train.

"Coming from the direction of town," remarked Gordon. "Short train and travelling fast. Wonder what all the hurry's about? They don't usually make that speed over this new line."

Slade was eyeing the skyline ahead. "Shore must be busy up there," he commented. "Look at the smoke they're making. Have they got big shops going already?"

"Why, no," replied Gordon, staring in his turn at the clouds of black smoke rolling up beyond the more distant hills. "I never saw smoke like that up there," he added, his grizzled brows drawing together. "They have a number of stationary engines and hoists and such things going, and several locomotives are usually busy in the yards, and it's a big camp. But that smoke—just look at it boil up!"

Slade's rejoinder was to quicken the pace of his big black.

"I've a notion we might be missing something int'resting," he said as Gordon's horse drew up alongside.

Gordon nodded and they increased their speed still more. Neck and neck they sped along the rocky trail. Gordon's eyes were fixed on the ominous smoke cloud, but Slade's keen eye swept every inch of the territory over which they were passing. It was his quick glance that first noted the still form huddled in the dust of the trail ahead.

The trail now wound through a straggle of growth, with a steep slope dropping down on the right and a jut of hillside on the left. Ahead the growth abruptly became a bristle of dense chapparal, and it was at the edge of this thicket that the figure lay. Over to one side stood a horse with patiently hanging head and trailing reins.

Gordon saw the form in the dust an instant later. "Look," he exclaimed. "That fellow must have gotten hurt! Looks like he's dead!"

He urged his horse forward, his attention fixed on the huddled form, but even as he did so an iron hand gripped the black's bridle and jerked his head sideways with a wrench that almost threw him. At the same instant Slade swerved his black sharply to the right.

"On, Shadow, on!" he thundered.

He hauled Gordon's snorting mount after him

as the black horse plunged down the slope. The black squealed shrilly as smoke and flame roared from the silent thicket, buckshot stormed through the air and a leaden pellet nicked his rump. From the tail of his eye, Slade saw the "dead" man roll over and surge to his feet, gun in hand.

Again the shotguns roared, but the blue whistlers swished harmlessly through the growth, a yard behind the fleeting pair. The frantic horses tore down the slope a full two hundred yards before they could be brought to a halt, panting and blowing, in a patch of mesquita rising higher than their heads.

Slade swung lithely to the ground, motioning Gordon to do likewise. The salonkeeper appeared dazed and bewildered and obeyed in a mechanical manner. He started to speak, but Slade held up his hand for silence. Straining his ears, he thought he caught the patter of swift hoofs silencing into the distance, but he could not be sure.

For long minutes he stood without sound or motion; but only the heavy breathing of the horses and an occasional nervous pawing on the part of the black was to be heard.

"I've a notion they've hightailed," Slade remarked at last. "Anyhow, they're not coming down this way. You stay with the horses and I'll see what I can find out."

Before Gordon could protest, the Hawk slipped noiselessly into the growth and vanished.

Wraith-like as a hunting wolf, Slade drifted up the slope, taking advantage of every bit of cover, straining his ears to catch the faintest sound, his eyes to detect the slightest movement. Finally he reached a point no great distance from the ominously silent thicket and crouched for long minutes behind a boulder, peering, listening. Between the thicket and his shelter was an open space of a dozen yards.

Intently he studied the crest of the growth, saw a jay swirl down in a flash of blue and perch upon a twig, cocking bright and knowing eyes. For more minutes he watched the bird flirt about, undisturbed and unafraid. It disappeared amid the growth for an instant, then flew off up the slope.

"If there'd been anything in that clump of brush, old fuss-and-feathers woulda been yelling his head off," the Ranger muttered.

Unhesitatingly he stood up and strode across the open space. He reached the thicket, burrowed into it, paused at a spot where the growth had been crushed and trampled. Peering through a thin screen of branches, he gazed down the stretch of trail he and Gordon had travelled shortly before. He fingered a raw spot on a branch, where the bark had been scuffed off.

"One of them rested his shotgun barrel here,"

he muttered. "Quite a hole-up. Six, seven of them, I'd say. Put that come-on jigger out there in the trail, figgerin' we'd stop and unfork to see what had happened to him. Then they'd have blowed us right out from under our hats. Nice little scheme, all right, and came mighty nigh to working.

"Question is, just how did they know we were coming along the trail right at this time? They couldn't have seen us in time to set the trap like they did. Shore musta had some advance information. Wonder who all Gordon talked to about taking this ride?"

The concentration furrow was deep between his black brows as he strode down the slope to where Keith Gordon waited with the horses. He recounted what he had found, as they rode back to the trail.

"But how did you catch on to it?" Gordon marveled. "I would have ridden right up to that fellow lying in the trail if you hadn't stopped me. It sure looked to me like he'd tumbled off his horse, or been shot off."

The flicker of a smile twitched the corners of Slade's wide mouth.

"Looked that way to me, too, for a second," he admitted. "But just in time I called to mind that I'd never before seen a jigger fall off his horse like that and lay with the brim of his hat pushed up and flattened out along the ground, and the hat still on his head. Feller would have to lie down easy and comfortable to keep his hat in place that way, and it seemed sorta funny to me for a feller to pick the middle of a dusty trail to corral a little shut-eye."

Gordon stared at him with admiration.

"You certainly don't miss anything," he applauded. "Man, you'd ought to be a detective or a sheriff!"

Chapter 6

Slade and Gordon rode warily through the thicket, but found no trace of the drygulchers. A half a mile farther on the trail forked, one branch heading due west toward the grim barrier of the Palomas. Slade rode along this branch a little way, intently scanning the ground. He turned and rode back to where Gordon waited at the forks.

"They went that way, all right," he said in answer to the other's look of inquiry. "Six or seven of them, travelling fast."

"Heading for the hills," nodded Gordon. "It's a regular hole-in-the-wall country over there, Slade. You're lost if you don't know the trails. An outfit like the Shotgun Riders could elude pursuit there for years."

"They'd be safe if they stayed in the hills," Slade agreed. "But their kind don't stay put. The bunch that drygulched us will be sifting back inter town 'fore the week's out, or before. Did you get a look at that jigger who was lying on the ground?"

Gordon shook his head. "I was too busy trying to keep Brownie from standing on his ear," he admitted. "Did you?"

"Sorta," the Hawk replied, "but 'bout all

can say for shore 'bout him was he had two ears and a nose, the forked end was down and there was a hat on the other end."

Gordon chuckled. "That's not too much to go on," he smiled.

"But I've a notion the jigger got a good look at me," Slade remarked gravely.

"Meaning?"

"Meaning that the next time he sees me, he may sorta give himself away."

"Fine," Gordon agreed, adding dryly, "but I've a notion, where one of that outfit is concerned, you'd better see him first."

"I mean to," Slade replied briefly.

Gordon stole a glance at the bronzed face, which was suddenly bleak, the eyes the color of snow dusted ice, and refrained from comment.

"Three times they've made a try," Slade muttered under his breath. "Three tries, and three misses. They're shore a willing lot of little jiggers, anyhow. But slipping up all the time like this is liable to sorta make them impatient, and impatient jiggers have a habit of tipping their hands."

Aloud he suddenly exclaimed—"Say, that smoke is thicker'n ever!"

Gordon stared at the rolling cloud, now appearing to mushroom up just beyond the next hill, and muttered something inaudible.

"The camp and the mouth of the valley are just

beyond that next ridge," he said a moment later. "We'll soon learn what's going on."

They pushed their horses up the slope, topped a final rise and uttered sharp exclamations as they stared at the scene in the valley mouth below.

The valley mouth was not very wide, Slade immediately saw, less than two miles, and for several miles it ran thus, a narrow gut between steep and rugged slopes. A few miles to the north, however, it opened out like a giant fan. The slopes north of the gut were much more precipitous, but a good ten miles separated their craggy walls. The gut appeared almost level, a rich green expanse extending from wall to wall, treeless, shrubless, but with a most luxuriant growth of grass belly-deep on a tall horse.

All this Slade noted in a single swift glance. Then his attention centered on the broad expanse of prairie upon which the valley opened. Here, at the foot of the gentle slope down which they sped, lay the construction camp, or what could be seen of it through the rolling clouds of black smoke. At first sight the whole scene appeared to be a welter of leaping flame.

"There were great piles of creosoted cross-ties along the tracks," Gordon shouted, "and they're all on fire. Look, the new roundhouse is going up, too, and the half completed office building. Come on, Slade, sift sand!"

They raced down the slope, coughing as the acrid fumes assailed their lungs. The camp was a scene of mad but orderly confusion. The clang of pumps and the hiss of water sounded above the shouts of men and the crackle of the flames. Locomotives, blowers roaring, black smoke pouring from their stacks, had hose lines attached to their mud valves and were spouting streams of water and steam against the flames. Their injectors were wide open, pouring fresh water into their boilers, and grimed and sooty firemen labored madly to maintain the steam pressure.

When the steam gauge needle dropped too far or the water in the water glass reached a dangerous level, the mud valve was closed until steam and water mounted again. By this method, several streams were kept constantly playing on the flames.

The same system was employed with the blow-off valves of stationary boilers which normally supplied power for various machinery. Bucket brigades were functioning, and an ant-like stream of workers were removing stacks of ties and other combustibles from the path of the flames.

"Those jiggers are doing one helluva swell job!" applauded Slade. "Come on, feller, every pair of hands counts!"

Swiftly they secured their horses and plunged into the fray. Side by side with brawny track layers and husky gandy-dancers, Walt Slade did the work of two of their best, wrestling heavy crossties and ponderous beams, helping to shove loaded boxcars out of the path of the flames.

He clambered across greasy rails, dodging rumbling strings of cars kicked down the leads toward distant tracks by a raging locomotive that banged and bellowed and slid screeching on brake-locked drivers.

"Mon, and it's me phwat's sayin' ye're worth a dozen ord'nary lads," declared a giant foreman, wiping his grimed and sweaty face with the back of a hairy paw. "Drill, ye terriers, drill!" he bawled to his men. "D'ye want this b'y to put the shame to the lot of yez!"

Across the tracks suddenly sounded a wild shouting. A man came tearing up to the sweating gang.

"Bring your min, Casey," he yelled to the foreman. "Bedad, and there's a car of blastin' powder in that string on the spur over 'yond the 'rip'-track lead. If that goes up, the whole yard'll be blowed to glory. Git the rag out! The fire's all over thim cars!"

Pandemonium ensued. The switch engine roared past, rocking and swaying, belching black smoke and clots of fire from its stack, rattling over the switch points as it sought to clear the way and jerk the deadly car from the spur and out of reach of the flames.

"She's blocked!" bellowed Casey. "They'll hafta

move half a dozen strings to git to that spur. Drill, ye terriers, drill!"

He led the way across the yard, Slade beside him. They crashed the car door open and revealed the squat containers of blasting powder cleated in orderly rows on the wooden floor.

"Bedad, and the roof's already a-blaze!" panted the foreman as Slade swung into the car. The foreman clambered after him.

"Stay by the door," the Hawk ordered. "I'll sling the cans to you and you can pass 'em out to the men."

"Right!" roared Casey as a container came hurtling at him. "Grab this one, Tim! Git in line, out there! Drill, ye terriers, drill!"

Gasping and sweating in the hot gloom, Slade tore the containers from the place and hurled them to the brawny Casey. Fire was eating through the car roof and little questing flames came flickering down. Hot embers began to drop onto the metal containers.

"If there's a leak in one of them—" Slade muttered to himself.

He did not care to finish the thought. With aching arms he hurled can after can to the grim catcher in the door, and ever Casey's hoarse voice boomed encouragement to his men.

"We're whoppin' 'er! Drill, ye terriers, drill!"

One end of the car was cleared. Slade leaped to the other end and the battle went on. With a crash the roof over the end he had just vacated fell in, sending showers of sparks in all directions.

"Just in time!" bellowed Casey. "If he'd took tin seconds longer, lad, we'd all been gonners. Ye're a wonder! Drill, ye terriers, drill!"

Outside the switch engine boomed and thundered, working frantically to clear the spur and jerk the burning car out of where it could be spotted under the huge pipe of one of the other columns used to fill the locomotive tanks. That barrel-sized stream would drown the fire almost instantly.

And just as frantically, Walt Slade labored inside the burning car to clear the containers from the path of the leaping flames. One whole end of the car was blazing now and the heat was almost unbearable. It was a mad race against time, with death and destruction as the loser's forfeit. Faster and faster the heavy containers flew through the scorching air, and ever Casey's hoarse voice boomed his war cry.

"Drill, ye terriers, drill!"

A terrific crash, and Slade was knocked sprawling. Casey clutched at the door jamb to save himself, swore appallingly and then bawled an exultant whoop as brake rigging clanged and couplers strained.

The switch engine had cleared the spur and coupled onto the string. There was a booming roar of the exhaust, the ring and clatter of spinning drivers, then the steady grind of the great wheels gripping the sanded rail. The burning car began to move, slowly at first, but swiftly gathering speed. The air of its passing fanned the flames to a roaring inferno.

Slade and Casey leaped to the ground and ran across the tracks to safety. A moment later and the switch engine was on the lead and screeching to a stop. Couplers banged and jangled, brake shoes screeched against driver tires. With deft skill the engineer spotted the blazing powder car beneath the outstretched pipe of the water tower. A tense and waiting brakeman jerked the rope that opened the valve.

With a gurgling roar the huge stream of water gushed from the pipe. Followed a prodigious hissing and sputtering, and billowing clouds of smoke-streaked steam. Backward and forward the engineer jockeyed the car, permitting the stream of water to play upon it from end to end. The roaring and hissing died to futile sputterings. The fiery glow vanished and the glistening containers, streaming water, could be seen as the steam cloud thinned.

"And thot's thot," said Casey. He turned and solemnly shook Slade by the hand.

"Forty years I've worked with good min—braw and sonsy min—" he said, "but niver the mon I'm seen as was the likes of you!"

Chapter 7

The fire was under control, and swiftly dying out. Slade and Keith Gordon lingered at the scene of battle for some time and then walked across the network of yard tracks to the single office building left standing. Inside they found a nervous young man receiving reports. He had jumpy eyes behind thick-lensed spectacles, but a stubborn jaw. He nodded to Gordon.

"This is my new foreman," Gordon introduced. "Slade, meet Duncan Taylor. Taylor is the engineer in charge of construction here."

Taylor acknowledged the introduction with a quick jerk of his head. He gave Slade a moist hand to shake, but his grip was firm enough.

"A hombre of contradictions," Slade decided. "You never can tell which way this kinda cat is gonna jump."

Duncan Taylor waved to a wash basin and towels. "You fellows will want to get the black off you," he remarked. "I heard you did fine work out there. Please accept my thanks and those of the road. How did the fire catch? It didn't catch—it was set. Broke out in half a dozen places just after daylight, while the men were eating breakfast and things were at their slackest—night watchmen going off duty, day men with the sleep still fogging their brains."

"Any idea who set it?" Gordon asked through a coating of lather.

Taylor shrugged. "Your guess is good as mine," he replied. "Some of the elements that have been opposing the road ever since we started building."

"The Shotgun Riders, for instance," remarked Gordon.

Duncan Taylor gave a snort of derision. "The Shotgun Riders are the bugaboo of you people," he scolded. "I am of the opinion they exist only in your imagination. I have never seen one."

" 'Piece of shell upon my back, indeed!" murmured Slade behind a towel. "What I can't see, I won't believe!"

"What's that?" demanded Taylor.

"Just talkin' 'bout a new-hatched chicken," the Arizona Ranger explained mildly. "Some feller wrote a poem, 'bout one once."

Duncan Taylor stared at him in perplexity. "I don't read much poetry," he replied vaguely at length.

Slade smiled brightly, and said no more. Gordon Keith changed the subject.

"Still figuring on running the line through Cienaga Valley, and over the Black Quag?" he asked.

Slade saw Duncan Taylor's stubborn jaw jut forward. His jumpy eyes took on a glassy look.

"That's another of your bugaboos," the engineer cried. "What is your Black Quag? Just a bit of shallow swamp that a few trainloads of crushed stone will overcome. Why shouldn't I use a perfect route made to order for me. My specifications call for a ninety-foot grade, ninety foot to the mile. I can't get that through the Tonto Pass, or anything like it. Through that pass, heavy trains will be forced to double-head and, doubtless, to use a third engine as a pusher.

"That's expensive and calls for a slower schedule. By way of Cienaga Valley I get better than a ninety-foot grade. Why the Valley is nearly level! The slope from here to the northern mouth and west by way of Feather Canyon is negligible. The Black Quag! I'll run a million tons of freight across the lousy back of your Black Quag!"

"You may run a line across the Black Quag, but you'll never hold it there," Gordon told him with quiet insistence. Nothing can stand on the Quag. For a while, yes, but sooner or later the Quag swallows it. It's bottomless!"

Taylor laughed jeeringly. "That's what people ignorant of engineering principles believe about any swamp they've lost a cow in," he scoffed. "Don't you think I know my profession, Gordon? Do you think I leave anything to chance? We made borings of your swamp to learn for sure just what is below the surface."

He whirled toward an inner room. "Mr. Allison!" he called.

A chair pushed back and a moment later a tall and broad-shouldered man appeared in the doorway, a questioning look on his strongly featured blond face. Slade noted that his dark eyes were slightly red-rimmed as from lack of sleep.

"This is Allison, my assistant," Taylor introduced. "Frank, I want you to tell Gordon what the borings you made revealed."

Glancing from his chief to Gordon, Allison replied in a dry, matter-of-fact voice.

"A rind of grass-grown loam, a number of feet of watery muck superimposed on a shallow bed of quicksand which in turn rests on firm clay!"

"You see!" Duncan Taylor crowed triumphantly. "We have the borings on exhibition, if you care to look at them. Typical of a morass of this nature which owes its existence to a stagnant seepage of surface water and a slope too slight to encourage natural drainage. I've handled this problem before. Good crushed stone fillings, drains, substantial ballast. Nothing to worry about."

There was a slight edge to Keith Gordon's silvery voice as he asked another question.

"Did you bore past the clay?"

"Not necessary," retorted the engineer. "Such clay extends to an indefinite depth and is usually firmly based on bedrock. Anyhow, we're not anchoring piers for a giant bridge or sinking the foundations of some huge building. The clay bed will provide all the support we require. Isn't that right, Allison?"

The assistant engineer nodded; his eyes, startlingly dark in his blond face, rested for a moment on Keith Gordon's ugly face, a flicker of contemptuous amusement in their depths. Neither he nor Duncan Taylor paid any attention to Slade during the course of the discussion. Which was not strange. After all, a roving cowboy could not be expected to have any understanding of the principles of engineering.

In which conclusion, however, they were very much in the wrong. When the unexpected death of his father occurred, following on the heels of business reverses that had cost the elder Slade his prosperous ranch, Walt Slade was in his third college year, pursuing the study of civil engineering. The urge to avenge his father's murder by wideloopers had sent him into the Arizona Rangers, which he quickly realized was going to be his life work.

However, he had never lost interest in the engineering profession. Continued study, and not a little practical experience in the course of his Ranger activities, had endowed him with greater knowledge and ability than many a man who boasted a diploma. In consequence, he followed the present discussion with no little interest, but without comment.

"You will lose your filling and your railroad," Gordon declared positively. "It may stand for a time, but sooner or later it will vanish. Nothing can stand on the Quag."

Taylor threw out his hands in mock despair. His expression was that of the astronomer who is assailed by a flat-earth fanatic. Then a smile flickered across his clever, bad-tempered face. He patted Gordon's shoulder in a friendly fashion.

"All right," he said. "I don't mean to be offensive, Gordon. After all, this is only a matter of business and a difference of opinion. When we prove to you that we are right, I know you will be the first to admit it."

"Yes," agreed Gordon, "when you prove it. In the meanwhile, I, and the other boys who put up the money to finance this venture are going to go broke. And," he added grimly, "Wade Thornton and the Cienaga Bank are going to have a lot of secondhand cattle outfits to manage. Our spreads are mortgaged to the hilt, Taylor."

"Six months from now, you and your associates will be making money so fast you won't know how to spend it," declared Taylor. "We'll run our road across your bugaboo of a Quag and west to the mines in record time. And by the way, Gordon, get us a herd of cattle down here in a hurry. We lost most of our meat reserve in this infernal fire. Talk about losing money! It keeps me busy writing vouchers for you, you old Midas. You're already getting rich before the road is half built."

Gordon shrugged resignedly. Argument was plainly futile with this nervous, stubborn optimist.

"I only hope I am wrong and you are right, but I'm sure skeptical," he said as he shook hands with the engineer.

Taylor smiled tolerantly, but from the tail of his eye, Slade noted an expression of derisive contempt again flit across the placid features of Allison, the assistant engineer.

"That big jigger doesn't 'pear to take much stock in anything Gordon says," he mused. "Well, Gordon's contention does sorta reflect upon his judgment as an engineer. After all, *he* made the borings, and I've a notion he did most of the field work of running the survey."

Before they left, Taylor turned to Slade and again warmly shook hands.

"Your work in that burning powder car was magnificent," he complimented. "If it hadn't been for you, there would have been a disastrous explosion, and, without a doubt, lives lost. Drop in and see me whenever you are at the camp. Incidentally, I intend writing a letter to the directors of the road, and another to Mr. Dunn, the General Manager, who, I hope, will be on

78

the ground before this line is finished. I am sure you would like Mr. Dunn, and he you."

Walt Slade smiled fleetingly as he shook hands and thanked the engineer. He did not see fit to mention that he, Slade, was personally acquainted with General Manager James G. "Jaggers" Dunn, the guiding genius of the great C & P system; and doubtless Duncan Taylor would have been vastly astonished to know that the famous railroad official numbered this tall, quiet man with the level gray eyes among his closest and most respected friends.

Slade and Gordon secured their horses and rode in a northwesterly direction. The trail did not enter the valley, however. Instead it veered more and more to the west, then turned sharply north and climbed the slopes of the low hills which flanked the valley. On the lip of the slope which tumbled steeply to the valley floor, Gordon reined in. He indicated the lush, green expanse below by a wave of his arm.

"There," he said, "is the Black Quag."

Slade gazed with interest. "Looks like green would describe it better," he hazarded.

Gordon shook his head, his ugly face brooding. "Green grass grows on a grave," he said, and was silent.

Slade continued to gaze down the slope, and as he gazed, the spell of the Quag settled upon his spirit like a chilling mist. That lush green, he now saw, had a deathly look. It was *too* green—like the green of a mouldering corpse, or the green of the scum that floats on the still surface of a poisonous pool.

No animal, large or small, trod the level expanse. No bird flew over it. Not even the writhing progress of a reptile rustled the tall grass which, apparently, had never been cropped by grazing horse or steer. Even the wind seemed hushed in the silent gut between the tumbling slopes. Only the drone of the distant construction camp broke the silence, and that seemed very very far away.

"And it *is* a grave!" Gordon exclaimed suddenly. "The earth beneath that grass is black as night, and God only knows how much of life it has swallowed. The Quag never gives up its dead! Do you want to hear about it—how it was first discovered? Perhaps you'll think it only legend—a myth—as Duncan Taylor does, and that the other yarns about it are grossly exaggerated, as he believes. But I'll wager you find it interesting."

Slade nodded, and as they jogged steadily along the trail that bored northward through the hills, he listened, with interest indeed, to the grim and weird story of the Black Quag.

Chapter 8

Don Martin de la Cara, recently knighted for bravery in battle by the Spanish King, was of sturdy peasant stock. No scented courtier of Leon or Castile was this squat, brawny soldier with the broad and placid face and the dreamy blue eyes, and only those who had seen him, an iron giant raging in the van, knew how strong and terrible a warrior he could be.

Don Martin haled from the high tableland of bare, sterile hills and rushing streams that looks down upon the broad blue Ebro, and hard beside the wild places of Navarre. There was little peace on that wild border, and before his soldier days, Martin de la Cara was won't to reap his scanty crop with sickle in one hand and sword in the other.

But nevertheless, his heart was rooted deep in the soil, stony and profitless though it was. He loved the good brown earth and did not grudge the toil required to wring a living from it. But like all men of his breed, *Don* Martin longed for a rich steading. And so, when the grateful king opened wide his bounty and asked what royal gift he should bestow upon his faithful liegeman, the dandified courtiers and the belted knights murmured their amazement when *Don* Martin requested a grant of land in the wild and fabulous New Spain, so far distant beyond the sullen waters of the broad Atlantic.

But the king, who also came from not too distant ancestors who had sprung from peasant stock, understood, and readily granted the request.

Almost without precedent was the grant bestowed. "From the eastern shores the waters wash, to where the sun sinks in the west, wherever he shall wish to till the soil and build; across to the number he shall desire," ran the royal writ.

Don Martin and his band of sturdy followers wandered across New Spain. West and north they journeyed, through *Mejico*, and into the land which later was to be known as Angora. And one day, as the sun slanted down the western sky, they came to the mouth of a wide valley.

The mouth itself was not wide, not nearly so wide as the valley farther north, but the soil was of unbelievable richness. How *Don* Martin chuckled with delight as he cut through the grass with his sword and dug his fingers into the fat, black earth. He visioned sunny cornfields, smiling vineyards, branches bending low with their weight of luscious fruit, flocks of fleecy sheep grazing in sheltered places. He turned a smiling face to his followers.

"Here is the place appointed," he cried. "We will wander and seek no more. Here will we build, and till the soil, and sit us down and take our ease."

Sturdy trees grew in profusion above the slopes that hemmed in the silent valley mouth where no tree grew, where no beast wandered. There was stone aplenty to be squared and shaped. The long train of pack mules which accompanied the wandering Spaniards bore all needful tools and supplies; but as the walls of his *hacienda* rose, *Don* Martin sent men southward time and again for rich furnishings, for rare and costly wines with which to celebrate the completion of the work.

And meanwhile *Don* Martin marveled at the richness of the soil here in the sheltered gut of the valley. He wondered why none had before now come to claim this jewel set amid the hills. Back in the mountain, and on the rolling land farther west, peaceful Indians sowed their grain on land not near so fruitful; but then the ways of savages were beyond the understanding of civilized men. *Don* Martin shrugged with Latin expressiveness, and gave the matter no further thought.

As the year drew nearer to its close, heavy rains fell and water rushed in torrents down the slopes; but it did not stand in pools upon the land. The thirsty soil drank it without sign of satiety. Only, the grass acquired a deeper green and wantoned more lushly over the black earth.

The *hacienda* was completed, and the huge barns and other buildings. They clustered together in friendly fashion upon the level ground.

"Later we will build a wall about the whole, but that can wait," said *Don* Martin. "Now we will hold *fiesta* in honor of that which we have accomplished."

During the busy day all was made ready. There was much wine, and good food aplenty. There would be music and song and dancing. All was cheerfulness and bustle.

Only once was a discordant note sounded, and that ominous note was sounded by the dreadful voice of the earth itself. It began as a distant mutter, far down the valley, grew to a seething rumble and a deep and terrible roar interspersed by vast sibilant hissings as from some mighty serpent prisoned deep in the soil. None knew it, but it was the warning voice of the Black Quag.

But the sound ceased quickly and was not repeated, and the warning went unheeded. Startled men laughed a moment later at their sudden fears. *Don* Martin gestured southward with a broad hand.

"Remember the fire mountains we saw in the course of our journey," he said. "The earth shook when they were aroused. Doubtless the earth shakes again, far to the south. It will not harm us here."

The sun sank in scarlet and gold behind the

western crags. The dusk sifted down from the mountains like blue dust. Many candles were lighted, and fires, for the air was sharp, and the rich glow shot wide bars of ruddy gold through the windows of the *hacienda*.

The cattle were cared for and munched their fodder in content within the comfortable barns. Night brooded over the dark valley like a nesting bird, and the stars that looked down from the black velvet of the sky seemed to shudder away from the deathly silence of the green-floored gut.

But inside the *hacienda* all was joy and light. Toasts were drunk, vast quantities of food were consumed. There was laughter, song, the clatter of busy knives and the clink of equally busy glasses. Finally the tables were pushed back, music filled the air and the dancing began.

Miguel Cortez was the most graceful and agile of the dancers. His leaps were higher, his pirouettes the longest sustained. But it was Miguel who slipped and fell heavily.

His comrades roared their laughter, but Miguel rose with an injured air.

"The floor," he complained. "It is not level."

Don Martin's pride was touched. "Silence, drunken one!" he thundered. "It is thy befuddled head that is not level. I, *Don* Martin de la Cara, laid this floor. It *is* le—"

The word died unspoken on *Don* Martin's lips.

Silently, with bulging eyes, he stood and stared. The floor was *not* level! It tilted at an angle, and as he stared the angle increased in sharpness.

Roaring an oath, *Don* Martin rushed to the door and sought to fling it open. It resisted his efforts, sticking fast between the jambs. Finally *Don* Martin summoned all his mighty strength and tore the door open with a rasp of splintering wood and a screech of warped hinges. Choking with unbelief he staggered back, staring wildly at a wall of black earth waist-high, that blocked the opening—a wall that slowly rose higher as the doomed building tilted more and more.

Don Martin roared a warning to his followers, and dived at the diminishing opening. The last man was dragged through a narrow crack, the heavy lintel-beam scraping hard against his back.

Madly the company fled away from the sinking building, their ears ringing to the terrified bawling of the cattle in the sinking stables.

They were too late to save cow or horses, for even as they paused with staring eyes and blanched faces, the peaked roofs vanished with an awful sucking and gurgling sound.

Overhead a full moon cast down her silver beams, and in the pale light was to be seen wide circles of black and rippling muck washing sluggishly against the fringe of black and crumbling earth.

"*La Cienaga Negra!*" *Don* Martin muttered. "The Black Quagmire! Comrades, let us be gone from here. This is a place accurst!"

"And that is how the Quag got its name," Keith Gordon concluded. "That is the story that came down through the years, scoffed at by some, believed by others. There are other stories, stories of those who scoffed, and dared to build upon the Quag. Stories of cabins that sank silently in the night, taking with them the sleepers in their beds. Stories of men who crossed the Quag and without warning were sucked down.

"When I was a boy, a whole herd of cattle was lost as the earth suddenly opened. Finally this end of the valley was left severely alone. Men began using this trail that detours through the hills, although it is hard drive for a herd; but better than to take chances with the Quag. You never can tell about it. At times it seems perfectly safe.

"The railroad surveying parties have passed back and forth across it time after time, on foot and on horseback, and nothing has happened. They even crossed it in wagons loaded with supplies. But sooner or later the Quag will claim its victims. They may be able to build the railroad across it, but the Quag will take it in the end. I can't make Taylor or Allison believe me, nor can other oldtimers around here. True, the Quag hasn't claimed a victim for many years, not since

I was a boy, but that is because residents here-abouts keep off it."

"It is part of yore holdings?" Slade asked thoughtfully.

"Yes," Gordon replied. "I have thought of forbidding the road to cross it, but that would do no good. They would invoke the right of Eminent Domain and acquire their right-of-way, anyhow. I have refused to accept payment for the right-of-way, though," he added grimly; "it would be blood money, sooner or later."

Slade turned in his saddle and gazed back at the green floored gut they had passed.

"I rec'lect a place somewhat similar over in Graham County," he reminisced. "It was a bog in a valley. A creek ran along one wall of the valley and water seeped through porous rock into the bog. Anything that got onto the bog was liable to be swallowed up—thin places most anywhere, and nothing to indicate them. First class land, too. Finally a girl came to own the spread that included that section. She was a smart little tike. She figgered out what was making the trouble, dammed the creek above the valley and turned it into a new channel. The bog dried up and she had one of the finest pieces of land you ever laid eyes on."

"That won't hold good here," Gordon pointed out. "There are no streams in this end of the valley, and no water running this way. The slope of the valley is to the north. The only water that gets onto the Quag is surface water running down the slopes when it rains."

"Is the Quag any different after a hard rain?"

Gordon shook his head. "Grass a little greener, is all. Surface water vanishes pronto. I have heard of sinkings occurring after months of dry weather. The only thing that ever presages a sinking, I have been told, is a rumbling sound deep down in the earth, and that doesn't always occur. In fact, I rather believe that part of the yarn is imagination."

"Well, if there is a firm clay bed beneath the muck the railroad shouldn't have any trouble," Slade predicted cheerfully. "I gathered from what Allison said that the mud and quicksand are of no great depth as those things go, and can be filled."

Gordon shook his head. "I'm afraid they are very much wrong," he replied. "When that herd was lost, when I was a boy, men probed with long poles and tried to find bottom in the hole that opened up. They couldn't even touch one of the cattle. Then they put a heavy weight on a long line. The line paid out nearly eighty feet, and stopped.

"They thought they had sounded the depths then, but somebody suggested letting out another fifty feet of line and then buoying it with a big skin filled with water, which only the heavy weight on the end of the line could sink. They left it all night, and when they came back in the morning, the skin had vanished, and they couldn't locate *it* with a long pole. And Taylor talks of filling the Quag with crushed stone!"

"Sounds like those fellows might have hit a deep hole or spring," Slade commented. "Chances are the rest of the place isn't like that. Do the holes always skin over?"

Gordon nodded. "Appear to. None in sight now, you'll notice; but I wouldn't care to walk across one of them."

As they approached a bend in the trail, Slade again turned to glance back at the Quag. A red sunset was storming above the Palomas and as the level rays of light poured like water over the serried battlements and spires, the long gut seemed filled to the brim with slow blood. Practical-minded and level-headed as he was, Walt Slade experienced a sudden cold that was not born of the swiftly falling night.

Chapter 9

Slade and Gordon reached the latter's Slash K spread after dark. Slade met the Slash K cowboys, and formed a good opinion of them at once. He likewise formed a good opinion of the spread the following morning. It was not very large, but the range was good—sufficiently wooded and plentifully watered, with cool canyons slashing the valley walls, in which dogies could find shelter from the hot rays of the sun in summer and from the icy blasts and drifting snow in winter. The ranch buildings were tight, well planned and in good repair.

"You have a nice little outfit here, feller," Slade congratulated his new employer. "Are all the spreads in the valley equal to this?"

"Most of them about the same," Gordon replied. "The XTI down at the lower end of the valley has its northern section cut up by some mighty bad canyons. Thorne loses steers into them now and then, particularly in *La Entrada Enfierno*—Hell-Mouth canyon. It's one awful hole, and when a beef falls into it, I guess there's nothing left but hamburger. Nobody has ever been down in there to find out."

"Thorne? You mean Wade Thorne, the banker, feller I met in yore *cantina*?"

"Yes. He owns the XTI. He's liable to own the Slash K, and a lot more spreads first thing he knows, although he doesn't think so. Thorne is, comparatively speaking, a newcomer in this section and is inclined to take the stories about the Quag as a pretty good joke. He sides with Taylor and Allison and doesn't appear worried about the money he loaned us on our spreads. He's liable to sing another song when he finds out he's in the cattle business up to his ears. He took over the XTI for a debt and I don't think he's been over pleased with his bargain, although the spread hasn't lost money."

"Thorne isn't a cattleman, then?"

"Oh, he has been, but then he's been most everything, I figure, though you wouldn't think so to look at him and hear him talk. He knows more about mining than lots of oldtime prospectors. In fact, it was Thorne who first maintained that there should be some lowgrade ledges in the hills west of here and that they could be worked at a profit, especially with a railroad running through this section. He grub-staked a couple of old jiggers and owns an interest in one of the mines. Seems to have considerable knowledge of geology.

"He once told me that he had prospected in South America. I gathered that he made money down there. Anyhow, he was able to take over the Cienaga Bank when he came here a couple of years back. The bank was on its last legs because of bad loans and equally bad management. Thorne got control, put his own money in, and straightened things out. Bank has been doing all right ever since.

"Well, I've told the boys to get busy on that trail herd for the camp. You look things over and get the lay of the land. Take charge when you're ready to. I've got to get to town, but I'll be back tomorrow night."

He was turning to ride away when Slade stopped him with a question.

"Who all knew you were figgering on riding out here with me yesterday?" the Ranger asked.

Gordon meditated. "Why, nobody, I guess," he replied. "I didn't mention it to Ward, my head bartender. He and Bill Cook, the day man, look after things when I'm not around. They are good men and can handle the *cantina*'s affairs without any difficulty. I am rarely there except at night. No, I didn't tell Ward. I—hold on! Recollect now, I *did* mention riding out here and that you were going along so as to take charge of the spread."

"To Ward?"

"No. After you left the *cantina* after the fire in Doc's office, I took the payroll money to the bank. Thorne locked it in his office safe—there's a watchman at the bank and we figured it would be safer there until morning, when the vault would be opened. I told Thorne I wouldn't want it until I got back from the spread."

"Anybody besides Thorne present when you mentioned us riding out here?"

"Yes," Gordon nodded. "Clate Shaw, the deputy sheriff, walked to the bank with us. He was in the office while Thorne and I talked. What are you driving at, Slade? Do you mean you think somebody tipped that gang off to our ride and had them lay in wait for us?"

"Well," Slade replied, grimly, "if somebody didn't, those hellions shore did a tall job of good guessing!"

Gordon swore angrily. "Clate Shaw's the man," he declared with emphasis. "Not that I mean to insinuate that Clate is tied up with killers and drygulchers," he hastened to add. "Clate is honest enough, after a fashion, but he's talkative, especially about folks he doesn't like, and he certainly has no love for me. Clate is in a sort of funny position, too. He got old Hank Bevins elected sheriff—campaigned for him throughout the county and lined up the tinhorn gambler vote, and the saloon hangers-on. He got a lot of wandering cowpokes and prospectors—hombres who claimed to be prospectors, anyhow—to the polls, and surprised everybody by getting Hank voted in.

"Of course Hank made Clate his chief deputy,

and Clate just 'bout ran the sheriff's office. I reckon Clate tried to do the right thing, but those fellows he lined up to vote for Hank have a habit of coming around, loafing in the sheriff's office, and so on. I'm of the opinion they always knew in advance every move Hank or Clate intended making.

"I lit into Clate hot and heavy several times about it, and so did Wade Thorne, but Clate is stubborn as hell and about all I accomplished was to get him on the prod against me. We finally had a good row and I reckon I lost my temper more'n I should have. I told him to stay the hell away from my place, and mostly he did. I'm not sure why Clate and Hank were in the *cantina* the night Hank was killed, but I gathered they were there to meet somebody."

"Any idea who?"

Gordon hesitated before replying. "I got this from Ward, my head bartender," he prefaced, "and Ward made me promise I wouldn't pass it on to anybody. I'm making an exception with you, and I don't want it to go any farther." He paused, and Slade nodded understanding as well as assurance.

"Ward and poor old Hank were pretty good friends," Gordon continued. "Ward got his information from Hank, in strictest confidence. If Hank hadn't gotten killed like he did, Ward wouldn't have mentioned it to me."

Slade waited in expectant silence and Gordon resumed.

"When the bank was robbed last week, Blackwell, the cashier, was alone in the bank; it was right at noon and the clerks and tellers were out eating. The robbers rode up to the bank, blew Blackwell's face off with a shotgun charge and cleaned the cages before anyone got there. They didn't have much time, however, and shots were fired at them as they rode out of town.

"Blackwell evidently struggled with his killers, for when he was picked up he had a black mask clutched in his hand. He had torn it from the face of one of the robbers. Well, Blackwell was dead and that didn't mean much. But—and here's where Ward's story comes in—it seems that a couple of days later Hank Bevins, the sheriff, got a letter, unsigned. It was an illiterate scrawl, according to Ward, but the writer said he was near the bank at the time of the robbery, and got a good look at the face of the man who lost his mask.

He wrote that it was the leader of the band, and he declared he could positively identify him and arranged to meet Bevins in my saloon. The bank had offered a big reward for the apprehension of the killers and I imagine the fellow had that in mind. He evidently didn't want to be seen going into the sheriff's office."

Slade nodded his understanding. "In a crowded

bar he could slip a few words to the sheriff without anybody noticing anything, while they were having a drink or playing the wheel or something."

"That's right," Gordon agreed, "but I'm afraid he didn't know Hank Bevins very well. Hank couldn't get his hand in a barrel without making a noise and would have been certain to give the whole thing away somehow. I imagine he did give it away, and doubtless that was why he was killed—trying to contact the fellow."

"How was he to know his man?"

"Ward said the fellow wrote he would wear a light-colored broad-brimmed 'J.B.' hat, a blue shirt with a dark-red handkerchief at his throat—regulation cowboy costume—and would light a cigarette right when the sheriff came in and looked along the bar. I've a notion he was there, all right, judging from the way Hank acted just before he was shot, but Ward didn't get a line on him, although he was keeping a watch, as he promised Hank he would do."

Slade made no comment, but instinctively his hand raised to the wine-colored kerchief looped cowboy fashion about his own sinewy throat. His lips pursed in a noiseless whistle.

"I told you this to show you how Clate is liable to act," Gordon concluded. "I've a strong notion he blabbed to somebody about the letter— a wrong somebody—and the word was passed on to where it would do the most harm. Anyhow, somebody laid in wait outside the saloon and cashed in Bevins before he could contact his man. Well, so long, I'm heading for town."

Slade voiced a final word of caution before Gordon rode away.

"I wouldn't have a row with Shaw over this," he said. "After all, we're not sure he tipped us off. Somebody might have watched us leave town and rode on ahead to pass the word."

"That's right," Gordon agreed. "I won't say anything."

Meditatively, Slade watched his new employer ride swiftly south.

"But if a jigger did see us leave town and managed to get ahead of us, he shore musta sprouted wings," he told Shadow. "It would take all day to skirt the trail and then work back up the slope, or I'm a heap mistook."

Meditatively, he fingered the handkerchief at his throat.

"Beginning to get a notion why those hellions have been after me so persistent," he mused. "The other night at the bar, I *was* wearing a blue shirt, and a red handkerchief; and, best as I rec'lect, I did light a cigarette just before the sheriff let out that yelp and started across the room. Funny, how things work out. Wonder what happened to the jigger he came there to meet?"

Walt Slade was to have the answer to that

question in the near future, and it was not a pleasant answer.

Slade largely shared the skepticism of Duncan Taylor pertaining to the stories about the Black Quag. He knew that such stories lost nothing in the retelling as they came down through the years. He knew that they were like to the yarns of lost mines, fabulous treasure and hidden hoards, with which the Southwest abounded.

It was only natural that in a region where there was much underground water, where rivers dived into caverns measureless to man and reappeared no more, where streams sank noiselessly through strata of porous rock and vanished, that tall tales would be told of bottomless bogs, of quicksands whose depths could not be measured and that swallowed whole herds of cattle.

Steers, plenty of them, had been lost in quagmires; and quicksand had claimed more than one human victim, but Slade had never met with a bog that could not be drained to provide firm foundations. Doubtless the Black Quag was but another such and with proper filling and draining would be safe as a right-of-way for the railroad.

Unlike Taylor, however, Slade's mind was open. Taylor based his conclusions on practical engineering experience, and those conclusions, so far as he was concerned, were final. Slade on the contrary, had encountered too many strange things and had seen too many apparently tall tales come true to be certain about any of them until he had personally proven or disproven them. He was ready and willing to admit that the Black Quag might constitute a much more difficult engineering problem than Duncan Taylor had any notion of.

But the Hawk did *not* share Taylor's skepticism where the Shotgun Riders were concerned. In the course of his Ranger experience, he had met up with more than one outfit of this nature. There was nothing new to him in their methods. Such bands almost universally relied on terror as their chief weapon. That was the answer to the shotgun killings.

A shotgun was the brand of the outfit: by murdering with a shotgun they impressed their power on men's minds. The Red Riders of the Enchanted Mesa country did it with red masks, he recalled. Knife work had been the distinctive trademark of an outfit he, Slade, had broken up on the Cochise Country. It was an old method, but it worked.

"They've got this section pretty well buffaloed already," he mused. "Folks who have evidence against them, who might even identify some members of the gang, are scairt to speak up. The jigger who witnessed the bank robbery was afraid to go to the sheriff's office with what he knew. And after seeing the sheriff murdered right before his eyes, I've a hunch he hightailed outa the country. Salty outfit, all right, and I've got very little to go on; but that kind allus make slips sooner or later. All we gotta do, hoss, is stay alive long enough!"

But judging from his recent experiences with the Shotgun Riders, Slade was forced to admit that *that* might be a considerable chore.

Slade quickly got the routine of the Slash K in hand. And the Slash K riders quickly realized that the new foreman was a hombre who knew every in and out of the cattle business. With amazing swiftness the trail herd for the camp was gotten ready. On the third morning after his arrival at the ranch, Slade told Keith Gordon that he would deliver to the construction camp the following day.

Gordon departed to carry Duncan Taylor the welcome news, for the camp was running woefully short on meat. Slade rode out with his men to comb a few more brakes and canyons where fat dogies were wont to hole up.

Late in the afternoon, after a successful roundup of suitable beefs, Slade rode alone down the valley. He had left the Slash K territory far behind and, judging from the brands he encountered, had passed over several small spreads. Far ahead he could see, stained scarlet and gold and amber and bronze by the slanting rays of the low-lying sun, a wild jumble of crags and spires, which, according to what Keith Gordon had told him, marked the northern end of the Cienaga Valley.

"Reckon that's where the bad canyons begin," he told himself. "They say that, aside from Feather Canyon, where the railroad aims to cut through, that there's hardly a one a steer can get into, unless he falls in."

Sitting his tail sorrel on a rise of ground, he swept the horizon with his keen gaze. The broken country to the north appeared to converge with the sprawling foothills of the Paloma range in the west, and this was of interest to Slade.

"Reg'lar hole-in-the-wall country to the nawth there," he concluded. "A prime hangout for the kinda gents who make up the Shotgun Riders, if there's a way in among those canyons and chimneys from the west hills. The bunch that tried to drygulch Gordon and me headed west inter the hills, that's certain.

"It's a plain trail they took, easy to follow, so it's ten to one there are places where they can cut away from it 'thout leaving a sign. They wouldn't go west, for that would take them into the big mountains of the Palomas, where the going is almighty hard and a bad spot to get caught with tired horses. To the south the hills peter out into desert, and Mexico is too far away to provide them a headquarters to operate from.

"Which makes it look like they'd be mighty apt

to head nawth. Of course they might steer more to the west and miss this section altogether, but it's wuth keeping in mind. Perhaps something will tie up with it."

He still stared into the north, his glance roving back and forth across the valley. Suddenly his eyes narrowed. High in the air and several miles distant were a number of black dots. Slade quickly placed them as condor vultures dropping slowly down from the upper air.

Condor vultures might mean several things. They might mean a dead animal of some sort; also they might mean a calf bogged down and unable to extricate himself, or a steer with a broken leg or other injury. And they might mean a man in trouble. Seldom, indeed, does a cattleman let a gathering of the fierce scavengers go uninvestigated.

"Reckon we'd better jog up there and have a look-see," the Ranger told his black.

At a swift pace he rode northward. Soon he ascertained that the vultures, many of them, were already on the ground, apparently attacking or feasting on something. He spoke to Shadow and the big horse increased his pace. A few minutes later and Slade could make out what had attracted the vultures.

They were crowding and jostling on the crest of a low rise, seeking to sink their beaks into something there. And as the Arizona Ranger drew near, he saw with a cold thrill of horror that the something was a man—a man spread-eagled on the hilltop by thongs that bound wrists and ankles to pegs driven deep into the ground!

Chapter 10

Grating an oath between his set teeth, the Hawk drove Shadow up the hill. He drew a gun and snapped a shot at a vulture perched on the man's chest. The heavy bullet slammed it head over heels, kicking and squawking amid a flurry of feathers. Its hideous companions arose with startled, angry croaks and flapped heavily away.

Slade pulled Shadow to a halt and swung down from the hull. He took two long strides toward the spread-eagled form, and then halted, a crawling nausea at the pit of his stomach. The man on the ground was horribly dead.

For long minutes the Ranger stood and stared at the mangled face from which the flesh had been nearly all shredded away, at the empty eye-sockets and the skull-grinning teeth. His gaze dropped to the thonged wrists, and he swallowed convulsively. Those wrists were caked with dried blood, and were so swollen that the blackened flesh completely hid the cords that bound them to the stakes—certain sign of a mighty and futile struggle on the part of the doomed man to free himself.

With a feeling of sick horror, Slade realized that the awful hooked beaks of the vultures had chiselled the eyes from the tortured victim's head and torn the flesh from his bones while he was still alive.

"The damn things will attack anything they see is hurt or helpless," he muttered, glaring up at the soaring vultures.

Slade turned his attention back to the mangled corpse. His lips tightened as he noted the ripped fragments of a blue shirt, and the shredded handkerchief, red in color, that was looped about the neck. The man was tall, slightly built. Of the face nothing could be made out, but the hair was lank and black. Slade noted with interest that the third finger of the left hand had been amputated, many years before, by the looks of the scar.

Setting his teeth, the Hawk squatted beside the body and went through the pockets. He discovered nothing of interest until he reached what was left of a shirt pocket. The find there, at first sight, appeared to be of no value. It was a crumpled wad of paper, stained with sweat and blood. With great difficulty Slade managed to smooth it out and decipher what was written upon it. His eye ran down a column of figures, carefully totalled at the bottom and signed "Mawson, Foreman, XTI."

Slade recognized it as a wage statement such as is given to cowboys by an outfit accustomed to advancing small amounts of money to its hands before regular payday. The statement was dated.

"The twenty-second of the month, that was the day before I landed in this section, the day before the sheriff was killed," Slade mused. "Less than a week ago. The jigger was alive on the twenty-second, and working for the outfit, or he wouldn't have gotten this statement on that day. Was tied on this hilltop some time yesterday or the day before, from the looks of him. Reckon he managed to twist and yell and scare those feathered hellions off for a while, until he got too weak; then they went to work on him."

He stared down at the dead man, who undoubtedly had been, very recently, at any rate, an XTI puncher.

And just as certainly, the Hawk knew, the body was the corpse of the mysterious informant who had endeavored to convey to Sheriff Hank Bevins his knowledge of the Cienaga Bank robbery.

"Those hellions found out about it, and this was their way of shutting his mouth," Slade growled. "Nice people!"

Grim and purposeful, Walt Slade rode back to the Slash K ranch. His mouth was still hard set the following morning as the trail herd was gotten ready for the drive to the construction camp. He watched the cowboys take up conventional positions for a safe and easy drive, and then he acted.

"Outriders on either side of the trail—way out," he told them. "I know it'll be tough going, but you've got to take it. Two scouts ahead one a quarter of a mile behind the other. Two rear-guard riders, same distance apart. *And keep yore eyes open!* We're up against an outfit we can't take any chances with. If I catch a man layin' down on the job, he'll answer to me puhsonally."

One look at the bronzed face, bleak as if chiselled from weatherbeaten granite, and at the level gray eyes, cold now as water torturing under frozen snow, and the cowboys obeyed without any arg'fyin'.

"Yuh'd think we was drivin' through old-time Injun country," one of the outriders grumbled to his bunky, but in low tones.

"Uh-huh," the other agreed, "but jest the same, that's jes the way I'm gonna act up on this drive. Yuh heard what that big ice-eyed hellion said 'bout answerin' to him puhsonally, didn't ja? Me, I'm scairt I mightn't have no right answers. Hit the brush, cowboy!"

With tired, scratched and sweaty rannies cursing fervently, but exultant, the trail herd roared into camp. Walt Slade saw the bawl-bellerin' dogies safe in corral and his riders s'rounding vast helpings of chuck in the cook shack. Before filling a plate himself, he went to the office. He found Duncan Taylor alone at his desk.

"Just in time," congratulated the engineer. "There would have been a lot of swearing around here in the morning if you hadn't gotten here today. Just to watch the way these rock busters can put away meat and whiskey is enough to give the average man indigestion and delirium tremens."

Taylor seemed to have trouble making out the voucher by which Gordon would receive payment for his herd.

"I'm sorry," he explained when at last he handed the somewhat blotted paper to Slade. "My regular glasses were broken a while back—Frank Allison accidentally sat on them—and I'm using an old pair that do not suit my eyes in their present condition. I require an unusual type of lens and of course it is impossible to get fitted out here. I leave most of the detail work to Allison and a clerk, but they are both in town this afternoon."

" 'Bout ready to start laying track again?" Slade asked as he stowed away the voucher.

"Yes," Taylor replied. "In a day or two now we shove out onto Gordon's bugaboo of a Black Quag. I don't expect to experience any difficulty, but I'm taking no chances and have assembled special equipment and extra steel piling. Like to take a look at it? I imagine this kind of work is a closed book to you, but perhaps you'll find the dredges and pile driving machines interesting."

Slade signified his willingness, and Taylor took him on a round of the camp, explained the purpose and functioning of the various machinery and materials. Slade listened gravely, with appropriate comment, displaying a mild curiosity that pleased the engineer.

"Over there is the machine with which we made the bores to test the Quag," Taylor remarked as they passed through a covered shed. "And in those frames beside it," he added, "are the samples the machine brought up. See— black, peaty soil, muck, sand, clay. You'll note the thickness of the clay layer—many, many feet—and of course we did not bore clear through to bed rock. That wasn't necessary."

Slade examined the borings with interest. Suddenly he bent closer, staring with slightly narrowed eyes. He examined several specimens, and when he turned to the engineer, there was a slight furrow between his black brows.

"Those borings went down a long ways, didn't they?" he remarked casually.

"Yes, straight down through the various soil layers and deep into the clay," Taylor replied. "Even an inexperienced eye can see that by bedding the fill on the clay and properly strengthening the fill with piling, and providing suitable drainage, that a solid and enduring roadbed will be provided."

Slade nodded, without further comment. As

they started to leave the shed, he asked a question.

"You say the big boss of this outfit is headed this way?"

"Mr. Dunn? Yes, we expect him before long. He is in Europe at the moment, but I was informed that he sails for America shortly. I hope to have steel laid far into Cienaga Valley before he arrives, however."

The air suddenly quivered to a heavy explosion.

"That's what's holding us up now," Taylor remarked, jerking his thumb in the direction of the sound. "We are driving drains into the mouth of the valley, and we are forced to do most of the driving through granite as hard as iron. A wall of it shuts in the mouth of the valley and goes down the Lord only knows how far. The slopes on either side of the valley are the same, incidentally.

"In fact, the valley is nothing but a giant trough with sloping walls and a V'd bottom of massive granite. That's the explanation of that swamp, in fact. While the surface drainage of the valley is from south to north, I am decidedly of the opinion that the drainage of the trough, and of the clay layer that fills the whole lower segment of the V, is from north to south."

Slade nodded agreement. "The configuration of the hills at the north of the valley would point to that conclusion," he remarked. "I noticed that the rock strata up there indicate a marked subsidence with a definite southward trend."

Taylor shot him a sharp look. "How the devil did you come to figure that out?" he demanded. "That's a geologist's conclusion."

"Oh, I've noticed sections of the country just like this one," Slade replied easily. "You get to notice things like that in the cow business. If you don't develop an eye for such things, you lose lots of steers in bogs and sinkholes and such. Come in handy, too, when you're digging water-holes or driving an artesian well."

Taylor nodded his comprehension. "The science of engineering is largely based on observation and the 'trial and error' method," he admitted. "Buffalo trails, for instant, gave our trans-continental lines many of their best routes and easiest grades through the West."

He led the way to the door of the shed. Slade, with a last searching glance at the boring samples of the Black Quag, followed the engineer to the open air.

"No, I'm not worried about the Quag," Taylor remarked; "but it's beginning to look like Gordon's notion of those Shotgun Riders he gabbles about might have something to it, after all, and that *is* something to worry about."

Slade noted that the engineer's faulty eyes were jumping nervously behind the thick lenses of his glasses. His face twitched, but his big jaw jutted forward stubbornly.

"They can't stop the road, though," he declared, "no matter what they do, and they did plenty of damage the other day."

"Meaning?" Slade prompted casually.

"I'll tell you about it," Taylor said. "The evening after the fire here in the yards, after we had gotten it put out and things straightened up a bit, we discovered that a night watchman was missing. Naturally, all hands turned out to look for him. We found him, in a ditch at the lower end of the yard. He'd been shot between the eyes."

"Cashed in?"

"No," Taylor replied. "That's the remarkable thing about it. The bullet must have struck at an angle. Anyhow, it glanced up along his skull, ran along under the scalp and lodged above his right ear. He was conscious when found, although weak from exposure and loss of blood, but he was completely paralyzed and could not speak. The boys toted him up to the emergency hospital and the doctor went to work on him. Got the bullet out and the wound properly dressed and he began to come out of it. Doc said the bullet, lying under the scalp and slightly imbedded in the bone, was exerting pressure on a nerve center and causing the temporary paralysis.

"After he'd slept a while and taken some food, Andrews, that's his name, began talking. He said he was making his last round and as he was walking along the track he was shot from ambush. There is a thick growth close to the right-of-way down there. The track is embanked steeply and whoever was hidden in the growth would have had to elevate the muzzle of his gun. I imagine that is what caused the bullet to glance and saved Andrews's life. The shock knocked him off the track and into the ditch.

"I suppose the murderers saw the hole between his eyes and the blood on his face and decided he was dead. Anyhow they left him dying. But Andrews wasn't even unconscious after the first few minutes. He watched the gang fire the stacks of creosoted ties and the new office building, and saw them ride away to the south. He said they wore black masks and carried shotguns. What do you think of that?"

Slade did not reply for a moment. Then—

"Those jiggers tried to do for me a coupla times," he said, "and nacherly I'm sorta int'rested in them. Do you think I could talk to that feller Andrews?"

"Sure, why not?" Taylor agreed. "He's coming along all right and is allowed to have visitors. We'll go up to the hospital right now, before we eat, if you're a mind to."

"I'm a mind to, all right," Slade told him grimly. "Let's go."

They found the watchman sitting up in bed, his

wounded head swathed in bandages. He was pale and weak, but cheerful.

"Nope," I didn't see any faces," he replied to Slade's question. "They wore masks, all of 'em, and they didn't take 'em off. A dozen or so of the devils, assorted sizes and shapes. The feller who 'peared to be d'rectin' things was a big tall feller with broad shoulders. The eye-holes of his masks were a mite large and I did get a purty good look at his eyes when he was standin' over me lookin' down inter the ditch where I was layin'. They were mean lookin' eyes, sorta glittery like a snake's, and they were either black or mighty dark blue. Blue eyes look black sometimes, you know."

Slade nodded, and his own eyes were bleak, and had deepened to a smoky gray with what looked like little leaping flames in the misty depths.

"And they carried shotguns?" he asked softly.

"Uh-huh," the watchman replied. "Shotguns and big pistols in holsters. And when they rode away out of the brush, I noticed some had rifles in saddle boots. Yeah, they were shore heeled plenty."

The sun had not set when Slade and his men finished eating, so they decided to ride to town before returning to the Slash K. Slade found Gordon in his *cantina*. The owner was pleased with his foreman's report, but shook his head when Slade recounted Duncan Taylor's decision to start grading Cienaga Valley.

"He's stubborn as a blue-nosed mule," Gordon declared. "Mark my words, Slade, when his damned right-of-way sinks into the mud and disappears, he'll still insist that more fill is all that's needed. He'll go right ahead and do the same thing over. And I happen to know that the working capital provided for the new line is running dangerously low. When that gives out, the directors will call for more margin, and we haven't got it and can't get it. It will end with the investors in this section losing all they put into the venture, and their mortgaged property also.

"Wade Thorne isn't a hard man, but he will have very little choice in the matter but to fore-close this time. He has already granted one extension. You can't expect him to keep that up. His bank has no very large working capital and he can't afford to take too many chances. As it is, some of the boys are behind in their interest payments. I don't care so much for myself, for I still have my business here, which will make me a living, and there is nobody dependent on me; but folks like old man Hathway of the Circle H, Bronson of the C Bar B, who has several young children, Richards of the Bowtie, who is putting a boy through college—those people are going to be hurt.

"It will just about kill old Vance Hathway to

lose the Circle H. It has been in his family for generations. He was born on the spread, his wife and children are buried there, and he always expected to be. It's killing to take an old man's home from him, with its associations and memories."

Slade glanced at the ugly face of the saloon keeper, and all of a sudden it seemed to him that it was very, very beautiful—beautiful with the beauty of sincerity, truth, compassion, and that inner peace that only these can give.

"Nope, the Big Boss up top the stars doesn't pay over much attention to the wrappings, just so the goods inside are sound," he murmured to himself, "and that's as it had oughta be."

His own sternly handsome countenance was wonderfully gentle and his normally cold eyes were all kindness as he smiled down at the squat little man who made light of his own troubles and worried about those of his neighbors.

"Take it easy, oldtimer," he said, quiet confidence in his deep voice. "I got a notion things are goin' to work out all right 'fore we twirl the last loop."

Keith Gordon glanced up at his tall foreman, a grateful expression on his face.

"You're a strange sort, for a wandering cowboy," he said, his silvery voice not altogether steady. "Somehow you sort of drill confidence into a person." Then, with a sudden uncanny insight: "I've a notion those broad shoulders of yours are in the habit of carrying other people's troubles."

Slade smiled, but made no further reply.

"I sure wish old Jaggers Dunn, the C & P General Manager would get back from Europe and look into this mess," Gordon remarked wistfully a little later.

And Walt Slade, recalling his trip through the shed where the costly excavating and filling machinery and the boring samples from the Black Quag were stored, voiced fervent agreement.

"I shore wish he would, too."

Chapter 11

Gordon hurried away to greet some freshly arrived customers and Slade leaned against the bar, sipping his drink. He was standing in nearly the same spot he had occupied the night the sheriff was killed, and he instinctively glanced toward the rectangle of the open window. Only it wasn't open now, he noted with a quirk of his firm lips. The heavy shutters were closed. Evidently Gordon didn't intend to take any more chances with that dark alley behind the saloon.

"I bet he's got three bolts on the back door, too," Slade chuckled.

The big saloon was filling up fast. The bar was lined from one end to the other and four bartenders were busy sloshing whiskey into glasses. The roulette wheels were whirring merrily, and the tantalizing click of the balls blended in a derisive chuckle to mock the wrong guessers who bent intent faces over the table.

Several poker games were going in a quiet corner and the seriousness of the players told of the large stakes and open play. A young cowboy, a fistful of bills held high above his red head in one hand, while he rattled the dice in the other, implored the "gallopin' dominoes" to "please come on, 'little Joe'—my pinto hoss needs new shoes!"

There was a whirl and glitter of color on the dance floor, where the girls in their silken and spangled dresses clicked high heels beside the thumping boots of cowboy and miner. Red shirts, blue shirts, gray shirts, yellow shirts, with the flash of handkerchiefs of contrasting colors at the throats, weaved in and out like an animated rainbow. Guitars thrummed softly, fiddles squeaked and banjoes thumped in lively fashion. Now and then somebody bawled a song, or what was intended for such, in more or less time with the music.

"Big night, feller, big night!" Ward, the head bartender remarked to Walt Slade as he paused to give a whirl to his handlebar mustaches. "Payday at the mines over in the hills yest'day, and the boys are in for a bust. Most of the spreads paid off t'day, too, and the rannies are givin' 'er a whirl. Look, here comes the XTI outfit, jest in from runnin' a big herd up to the mines. That's Bunch Mawson, the foreman, in front. Bunch gets ugly when he drinks and there's liable to be trouble with that outfit 'fore the night's over. They stick t'gether, and keep to theirselves most of the time, too."

Slade glanced at Mawson with interest, recalling the name signed to the statement he had found in the pocket of the ill-fated puncher pegged out for the vultures to tear.

Mawson was a big hulking man with dark,

intolerant eyes, a bulbous nose and a bushy beard. He had a habit of wetting his lips with the tip of his tongue, as if they were continually dry. He shouldered his way roughly to the bar, his men wedging out behind him. Soon they had crowded themselves a place and stood shoulder to shoulder, downing prodigious quantities of straight whiskey and chattering among themselves.

Keith Gordon made his way back to Slade and ordered drinks for them both. As he held his glass up to the light before downing the contents, Slade spoke.

"Before I headed up this way from Cochise country," he remarked in tones of casual conversation, "I heard tell that a jigger I usta know down in Cochise was working in this section. We usta ride t'gether. I don't rec'lect his name—can't say for shore if I ever heard his real one: we allus called him 'One Short,' which us'ally got whittled down to Shorty. That was because he'd had the third finger of his left hand cut off right down to the roots. He was a gangling sorta gent with straight black hair. Ever hear tell of such a jigger?"

Gordon thought a moment. "Yes," he said at length, "I recall him now, because of the missing finger. He works for the XTI—I don't know his name."

He glanced at the XTI men lining the bar, and shook his head.

"Don't see him with the bunch up there. Perhaps he's on wrangling duty at the spread. Come on, we'll ask Mawson."

Bunch Mawson turned his flushed sullen face toward Slade as Gordon asked about the missing man and explained Slade's interest. Mawson raked the Ranger's face with his hot little eyes that were already bloodshot with liquor, but his rumbling voice was civil enough as he replied.

"Reckon you must mean Crip Bayles. You say you usta know him down in the Cochise and just landed in this section recent? Hell, you musta passed him on the way up. Crip quit the XTI 'bout two weeks back, said he was headin' back to the Cochise."

"Two weeks ago?" Slade repeated. "That musta been about the fourteenth. I was on the way up here on the fourteenth."

"Uh-huh, that's right, the fourteenth," Mawson agreed, nodding his bristly head. "I rec'lect now, it was the fourteenth. I made out his pay voucher and I remember datin' it the fourteenth. That's right, the fourteenth. Have a drink?"

Slade declined with thanks and he and Gordon went back to the end of the bar.

The night wore on, and the saloon became increasingly boisterous. The bar was crowded two-deep, more poker games were going on, men waited their turn at the wheels and the dancers on the floor could do little more than bump and jostle.

"Didn't I tell you she'd be lively?" demanded the perspiring Ward, giving his ferocious mustaches an extra twirl. "The boys are beginning to feel their oats and there's liable to be doin's 'fore daylight. The XTI crowd are steppin' high and handsome already and Bunch Mawson is headin' the pack."

Slade had already noticed that Mawson was getting very drunk. His speech was thick, his face red and mottled, but his hand was steady and his step firm. Mawson evidently could "hold" his likker.

It was making him increasingly quarrelsome, however, and more than once only the efforts of his somewhat more sober riders staved off a row. But the hands were fast reaching the same bellicose state as their foreman.

Slade watched the group intently. It was he who first saw the entrance of Wade Thorne, the banker, who was also owner of the XTI. Thorne instantly spotted the noisy group at the bar and walked precisely toward them, his clearly featured face wearing its eternal half smile, but with a little flicker of light in the depths of his brown eyes.

Bunch Mawson was hammering on the bar and shouting something in a thick voice when Thorne suddenly reached out a slim, white hand, gripped the burly foreman by the shoulder and whirled him about with a strength that belied his slight form. Slade could not hear what he said to Mawson, but the latter flushed a fiery red at the words.

"I ain't going," he bawled.

The little banker shook him, with a force to snap his teeth together. Mawson roared with anger and swung a blow with his ponderous fist. Thorne merely moved his head aside an inch or two, allowed the huge fist to whiz harmlessly over his shoulder and lashed out with a slim hand.

With a grunt, Mawson reeled back against the bar, blood pouring from a cheek laid open to the bone. Thorne stood motionless, the half smile still playing across his lips, the waxen fingers of his left hand gripping the left lapel of his coat. And at that gesture, Walt Slade stiffened for instant action.

For a moment Mawson glared at his employer as if dazed. Then his face flamed scarlet, he bawled an oath and went for his gun.

He was fast, damn fast! But before his big Colt cleared leather, Wade Thorne's right hand blurred whitely toward his left armpit, the fingers of his left hand jerking open his coat by the lapel. The room rocked to a report and Mawson went reeling back against the door, clutching at his blood spouting gun hand.

Wade Thorne's barrel, rock steady, still wisping smoke, lined with the foreman's heart. But even as Mawson stiffened to receive the impact of the heavy slug, and Walt Slade's long Colt flashed from its holster, Thorne apparently changed his mind. He sheathed his shoulder gun with the same graceful speed with which he had drawn it and addressed Mawson in his precise, correct voice.

"Get over to Doc Groves' office and get your hand attended to, and then head for the ranch, pronto!" he said.

Mawson's big shoulders drooped, his gaze shifted away from the glittering brown eyes of the banker. He stooped and retrieved his fallen gun, holstering it awkwardly because of the bullet wound in the fleshy part of his hand.

"Okay, Boss," he mumbled, "I didn't mean nothin.'"

He shambled toward the door. Thorne turned to the riders, who shifted uneasily under his glance.

"That last goes for the rest of you—unless you'd also rather visit Groves first," he remarked pleasantly. "Get out of here!"

They "got," without any arg'fyin', leaving half filled or untasted glasses on the bar. The banker watched them go, then, nodding pleasantly to acquaintances, he also left the saloon.

The crowd, which had been stunned to silence by the sudden and unexpected passage, broke into a gabbling roar; dance floor girls squealed hysterically as the reaction set in; bartenders uttered soothing yells.

Walt Slade leathered the long barrel that a moment before had lined with the banker's gun hand. He speculated the swinging doors, the concentration furrow deepening between his black brows. Ward, the head drink juggler, came back from examining a bullet hole in one of the "mahogany" panels of the bar.

"That banking gent sorta runs his outfit plumb up to the hilt," Slade remarked.

Ward nodded emphatically. "Ev'ry time I see that little jigger in action, I think on what an ol' feller who drifted in here 'bout a year back said," he observed pensively.

Slade looked interested, and Ward continued.

"He was an old rounder who'd drifted here from over back east. Thorne came in for a drink while he was gabbin' with me and the ol' feller, after givin' him a once over, asked who he was. I told him and he sorta shook his haid puzzled-like and opined that:

" 'Put a long black coat and a black string tie over a plumb white shirt on that feller, and he'd be the spittin' image of a Mississippi River steamboat gambler named Thornton I usta know. They called him "Draw an' Fill" Thornton, and he was the coolest hand that ever bluffed three-of-a-kind with a bob-tailed flush, or killed a

126

hombre who already had the drop on him. Yeah, he shore looked like that banker feller, only he was a heap younger and dressed dif'rent.

"When I think of what that ol' feller said, I get to wonderin' if lookin' alike makes folks alike in other ways, for Wade Thorne is shore one cold proposition, in spite of them salt-an'-pepper suits he wears and his way of talkin' like his mouth was fulla mush."

Slade nodded agreement, still staring at the swinging doors that had closed behind the banker a few minutes before.

"Where'd Thorne come from, you know?" he asked idly.

"From Dallas, Texas, I un'stand," Ward replied. "He come here well heeled with *dinero* and he had letters and rec'mendations from a big bank over to Dallas, the Drovers' Exchange, I b'lieve it was. He bought the XTI spread from the Davenport brothers, who wanted to pull out for Californy, and he got control of the Cienaga Bank when ol' Bruce Tolliver cashed in. Got a haid on him, that jigger."

For a little while the groups at the bar discussed the shooting, but soon the affair was forgotten in favor of more pressing matters, chiefly liquid. But Ben Ward, who alone of those around him had noticed Slade's lightning draw and throw-down on the banker's gun hand as the other lined his barrel with Bunch Mawson's heart, tugged at his mustache, and eyed the tall, gray-eyed man reflectively.

"And I've seed somebody what looks one helluva lot like *you,* big feller," he ruminated to himself—"jigger who was chain lightnin' on the draw but had plumb perfect control of his trigger finger, like what you just showed when you *didn't* shoot that gun outa Wade Thorne's hand to save Bunch Mawson's wuthless hide, 'cause you saw in a half of a split second that it wouldn't be nec'sary. Let me see, now, seems as I rec'lect I was drunk or suthin' that time. Let—me—see!"

Suddenly the bartender's eyes widened, his mouth dropped slightly and his mustaches seemed to curl of their own accord.

"By gosh!" he breathed in awed tones. "I ain't sayin' one damn word, even to myself, but I believe it is! Yes siree bob! It *is!* Well, if that don't take the rag off the bush! Gentlemen, hush! I don't know what this is all about, but there's gonna be doin's in this section! Yes siree! There's gonna be doin's!"

He stared at Slade for an instant longer, an awed look in his eyes, then his face became expressionless as he turned back to his multitudinous duties.

A little later, Keith Gordon joined Slade.

"Well, that was a close one," he remarked. "I reckon Bunch Mawson never was nearer a coffin than he was at that moment. Thorne is a

128

bad man to trifle with, and when he gives an order he expects it to be obeyed."

Slade suddenly turned the full force of his level green gaze upon the other.

"Gordon," he said softly. "Will you do me a favor, and not ask any reasons why?"

The saloon keeper smiled. "I'm not apt to hold out on a man who saved my life, perhaps a couple of times," he said with feeling, the bell notes ringing clear in his silvery voice.

"Fine," Slade nodded. "Get a pencil and paper and come into your office. I want you to send a telegram over the railroad wire—you can do that, can't you?"

"Yes," Gordon replied, and led the way to the locked back room.

A few minutes later he was staring with a dazed expression at the words Slade had written.

"You are a man of position in the community, a land owner and a business man," Slade pointed out. "They'll give you that information without question."

"But—but," stammered Gordon, "there can't be any question about *him*. Why do you think—"

"You mentioned you wouldn't ask any reasons why," Slade pointed out.

Gordon shut his huge reptilian mouth tight. "Okay," he said, "and I'll hold the answer unopened and unread."

Soon afterwards, Slade rounded up his men

and started on the long ride back to the Slash K.

"We've got another trail herd to get t'gether," he pointed out. "Duncan Taylor said he'd need more meat mighty soon, and he's depending on us to drop a loop on it.

"And I've got a little loop dropping of my own to do," he added softly to himself.

Chapter 12

Slade rode to the ranch and started the business of getting a second trail herd together the following day. Under his expert direction the herd was swiftly assembled. Finally all was ready for the drive. Slade eyed with satisfaction the fine bunch of fat beefs contentedly chewing their cuds near where a dark canyon mouth opened onto a little flat well grown with grass and watered by a small stream.

"Everything okay up to now," he told young Bart Clanton, who acted as his assistant foreman, "but you never can tell at this time of the year. Tell the night guards to keep their eyes open. I'll relieve you at midnight, and then get an hour or so of shut-eye after four o'clock. We want to make an early start. They're yellin' for meat down at the camp. *Buenas noches*, feller."

"If you'll promise to sing a mite to the critters after you take over, I'll stay up after you take over," Clanton remarked hopefully. "It's worth losin' shut-eye to hear you sing, feller."

El Halcon chuckled, with a crinkling at the corners of his gray eyes, but did not promise.

The night closed down. After a spell of yarning and singing, the cowboys took their bedrolls from the wagons, rolled them out on smooth patches of ground and went to sleep.

"Looks like a nice night, anyhow," Bart Clanton said. "Lucky we ain't had no storms."

Slade took his turn as night guard at midnight. His post was on the side of the bunched herd next to the canyon mouth. He could hear his fellow night guards singing as he rode Shadow slowly along the face of the herd. The night was breathlessly still with not even a gossamer-fluttering breeze stirring.

Suddenly to The Hawk's keen ears came a low mutter of sound, a vague, unreal vibrating of the air, it seemed. He glanced up at the golden spangling of stars overhead. They appeared a trifle misty, as if they were blurring through smoky window panes. His gaze traveled around the horizon, paused when it reached the northeast. A dark object seemed to be rising out of the ground. It rose with amazing swiftness, and as it did so, the misty stars were blotted out one by one.

"Looks like trouble," The Hawk muttered.

There was a sudden flicker of bluish light that raced over the dark surface, then another. The ominous mutter sounded again, louder, grew to a rumble. The black mass had reached the zenith and was tumbling down the long arch of the sky. A breath fanned Slade's cheek, an icy breath, as if a dead man had suddenly exhaled from his congealed lungs. He could hear the night herds further up the canyon calling to one another. Again the muttering rumble. Then without warning a blaze that seemed to split the black heavens into jagged streamers of flame. A deafening clap of thunder. Again the lightning blazed, and the thunder rolled. A wind came roaring down the canyon, crackling the tree branches, bending the grass heads curvingly toward the earth. There was a sound of activity from the neighborhood of the wagons. Punchers were storing their bedrolls, the cooks were putting their wood in out of the wet.

Slade was singing now, for the cattle were on their feet. By the almost continuous flash of lightning, he could see a sea of shaggy heads and gleaming horns all pointed in his direction. The steers were quiet as yet and he knew that, standing thus with their heads toward him, they might remain motionless despite the storm, if nothing happened to set them off. But he knew, also, that sometimes even a steer shaking himself will start the whole herd on a wild stampede.

The other night guards were singing to soothe the herd. Slade had struggled into his slicker and he bent his head to the sheets of rain and the pounding of giant hailstones. The cattle were getting restless. A vivid flash of lightning showed them coming toward him at a slow walk. So far so good. Wouldn't be hard to keep them together, to guide them.

The lightning blazed. Over to the left there was a vivid reddish flash and for an instant Slade thought the bolt had struck the herd. But the thunder clap did not follow quickly enough. Even before its boom, though, he heard a terrific bawl from a steer—a bawl of pain and fright. There was a milling and rushing, a clatter on the rocks, then the roaring pound of thousands of hoofs.

Slade wheeled his horse and rode. There was nothing else to do. He was racing in front of thousands of stampeded long-horned Texas steers, in as terrifying a position as it was possible to find himself. The steers were all around him, pressing close. Came a particular vivid flash of lightning and a roar of thunder like the rending of creations. The cattle reeled and shied. A mad rush, a roar of pounding hoofs, and Shadow was swept clean off his feet. Slade kicked free in the flickering instant of time vouchsafed him. The powerful black surged to his feet and Slade flung himself into the saddle.

"Trail, Shadow, trail!" he thundered. The great black horse leaped forward, shouldering steers aside, knocking some from their feet. He snorted through flaring nostrils, and the wind lashed his wet mane across Slade's face. On and on, with the lightning blazing, the thunder roaring and the bawl and bleat of the terrified cattle sounding thin and unreal above the pound of countless hoofs.

Slade was out ahead. He began riding zigzag fashion in front of the fleeing herd, seeking to slow them up and, if possible, start them milling. He knew that if they started to mill and got out of control, they would run in a circle faster and faster until they broke up into bunches and scattered all over the range; but he had to take that chance. Under foot, he realized, was the Coronado Trail, here wide from much travel. Ahead, and only a few miles distant, was grim Skull Canyon.

"I'll lead the hellions in there if I can't get them turned, and the shelter will slow them up, mebbe," he muttered. "Hell, I believe this damn rukus is stoppin' as quick as she come up!"

The rain had ceased abruptly. The wind was falling. The lightning flashes were less vivid, the darkness more intense. The cattle, too, were slowing. Then suddenly a yelling sounded off to the left and the steers quickened their pace.

"Have those jiggers over there gone plumb *loco?*" Slade demanded. He let out a roar of protest to the unseen noise makers.

"Shet up and ride 'round here in front!" he boomed at them.

There was an instant of silence save for the beat of the hoofs. Then a lance of orange flame split the darkness. Slade heard the vicious whine of a slug scant inches from his face. Another flash, and he felt the wind of that one. He ducked instinctively, for the instant bewildered. Then, as a third bullet yelled past, he jerked his gun and sent three quick shots at the flashes. There was a howl of pain and the sudden clatter of a racing horse.

"Winged him and creased his hoss," The Hawk muttered. "Now who in blazes was that?"

Abruptly the rain swished down once more. With it came sleet and pounding hail. A shriek of wind lashed *El Halcon*'s face, and he realized that this freak storm was cutting some more capers. The cloud had split and the whirling vortex had swung around. The wind now blew from exactly the opposite direction. Under its stinging lash, the herd slowed to a walk, milled, shambled, began to drift sideways. Gradually it turned, until the bawling steers were pounding back the way they had come. Slade chuckled grimly as he urged Shadow to greater effort. His first instinct was to get in front of the herd, where the cowboy belongs if he doesn't want to lose his cattle, but he realized that the steers were following the general trend of the trail. The shallow box canyon lay ahead.

"Looks like we're gettin' the breaks at last, feller," he told the black horse. "Funny things happening t'night, oldtimer, mighty funny things!"

On and on through the black dark and the blue glare of the lightning! Ahead suddenly gleamed a winking point, and another. Slade muttered an oath and jerked his gun. Those points of light, he knew, were the lanterns that marked the positions of the wagons. He fired shot after shot into the air to warn the cowboys. A moment later he heard the popping of their guns as they tried to turn the herd. There was a crash and a wild volley of yells as the stampede hit the wagons, turning two of them over. Then the herd went bawling up the canyon and a score of riders closed in behind them.

"Okay, pardner," Slade told his reeking horse. "They'll hold 'em now, and the storm's letting up, too."

Old Keith Gordon and the cowboys were loud in their praise of The Hawk the following morning.

"If you hadn't kept in front of them and kept 'em t'gether like you did, hell only knows where they'd be by now," the former declared. "I'd shore like to know what started 'em off. They were standin' fine, and then all of a sudden they was off. I wonder why?"

Slade wondered too, and all day as they cut out and branded he was trying to learn why. It was toward evening when his attention was attracted by a big wild-eyed steer with one broken horn. For several seconds he sat staring at the animal's hind quarters.

"Hair all singed and burned off up 'bove his hocks," he muttered. "Like somebody'd held a fire against him. Hell, there's just one thing could burn the critter like that! Powder! Somebody set off a charge of powder 'gainst his laigs. That's the funny red flash I saw just after that big lightning bolt. No wonder the pore devil started a stampede. He's burned raw."

He noted the position of the burn on the animal's legs and his black brows drew together. A leaping light birthed in his gray eyes.

"Funny," he muttered. "Funny place for that powder to be held. And that ties up with the other things I noticed. Yeah, the whole bus'ness is beginning to tie up, or I'm a heap mistook. Uh-huh, they deliberately started a stampede last night, figgerin' on runnin' the herd off during the storm. Darn nigh got away with it, too!"

The herd hit the trail for town, but Walt Slade did not ride with the cattle. Instead, he turned aside at the mouth of a dark canyon near which he had exchanged shots with the wideloopers the night before.

"That's Skull Canyon, feller," remarked Bart Clanton. "A mighty bad hole. Nothin' up there. Okay, if you want to take a look-see. Meet you in town."

Chapter 13

"We gotta find out how they figgered to get that herd in the clear 'fore they were caught up with," he told Shadow.

Skull Canyon was not very wide and was heavily bush grown. On either side the chaparral edged close to the trail and the progress of a herd would of necessity be slow.

Shadow clattered through a dry wash. On the right the growth straggled along the base of the cliffs, but to the left the bare wash curved toward the canyon wall. The trail itself was almost naked stone and little marked by passing hoofs.

A mile farther on Slade rode out of the south end of the canyon. Pulling Shadow to a halt, he lounged easily in the saddle and gazed northward toward where the unseen purple mountains of Utah rose. Over to the right, many miles distant, but showing plainly in the clear air, was a smudge of smoke that Slade knew marked the site of the railroad town.

With interested eyes he followed the only possible course the trail could take through the shouldering hills.

"Hell," he muttered, "the trail hasta pass within four or five miles of Clifton, up towards the line. How in blazes did they expect to run that stampede past there in broad daylight? They couldn't do it. There's a telegraph line from Cienaga to Clifton, and 'fore they could possibly get the herd that far, Clifton woulda almost certain been notified to be on the lookout for it. Shore looks like only a *loco* outfit woulda chanced it, and the outfit what's been raisin' the hell in this district shore hasn't got any earmarks of being *loco*. Now what's the answer? Easy! They musta figgered on holin' 'em up somewhere. But where? Must be somewhere 'tween here and back where they started the stampede."

With his mind's eye he checked over the route he had just followed, with barren results. Nowhere had he passed a canyon or draw that would have provided a hiding place for a herd of that size.

"But just the same, she's back there somewhere," he declared. "Feller, let's you and me ride back and see."

He turned Shadow and took the back trail, scanning every inch of the terrain. Again they clattered through the dry wash, climbed the shelving bank on the far side.

Suddenly Slade pulled the black to a halt. "Hold it, feller," he exclaimed in a tense voice. For a long minute he sat eyeing the growth to the left. Then he turned Shadow back into the wash and rode up the boulder littered bed. At the edge of the growth he swung down from the saddle. Now that he was near, he could see that here it lacked the fresh appearance of the foliage that flanked the wash. He stooped down, grasped a sizeable sprout with both hands and heaved mightily. The bush came out of the crevice in which, apparently, it was firmly rooted. Slade stared at the cut end with narrowed eyes. Then he carefully replaced the growth and straightened up.

"An old trick," he told Shadow. "Yeah, an old one, but a good one, and one that'll fool the av'rage posse ev'ry time. Pertickler a posse what's got reason to b'lieve the outfit they're chasin' is on ahead and steering for the line. You and me passed here on the way up without givin' any thought to this brush growing on the bed of a wash that's shore to be fulla water during ev'ry rainstorm. Chaparral doesn't take root and grow in water. If those owlhoots had been just a mite smarter and cut brush and stuck it in the rocks on the other side the trail as well as on this side, the chances are we wouldn'ta noticed even when we rode back this way looking for things. Yeah, owlhoots allus over-look some little thing like that. C'mon, feller, let's not you and me overlook anything!"

He rode back to the trail and down it for some distance. Then he sent the protesting Shadow straight into the thick growth. After a hard struggle they reached the base of the cliffs and found the going easier. A few minutes later and they hit the wash beyond where the cut brush had been carefully stuck into the crevices to simulate the flourishing growth. In the canyon wall was a wide opening which narrowed toward the top until from the trail it was not noticeable. This crevice bored into the hills. Its floor plainly showed the passage of many hoofs.

Slade rode into the crevice, every sense alert, tense, watchful. The narrow gorge wandered on through the hills, turning, twisting, with towering cliffs hemming it in on each side, their lofty crests drawing together until only a thin thread of blue marked the far-off sky. A greenish twilight shrouded everything and the sound of Shadow's irons was muffled and dull. And then abruptly the gorge widened, the tall cliffs fell back, curved sharply on either side and The Hawk found himself in a wooded canyon with the trail winding on between thick chaparral growth. And even as he pulled up the black to listen, to his ears came, thin with distance, the querulous bawl of a steer.

"We've hit it, feller," he told the black, "a reg'lar hole-in-the-wall hangout. I betcha you we find ev'ry steer what's been widelooped in this district for the past coupla months, mebbe longer. Run 'em off the range, snuk 'em in here and hole 'em up till a good stormy night and then slip 'em inter Mormon land. Smart outfit, all right. Take it easy, now. I got a big notion there'll be a cattle guard in here some place, and we don't wanta get our ears pinned back.

For some distance he followed the trail, the sounds of the cattle growing louder as he advanced. Suddenly he sniffed sharply. There was a fragrant tang of wood smoke coming from somewhere. Another hundred yards or so and he turned the black horse into the crush that flanked the trail.

"Here's where you pick up a few more scratches, feller," he apologized, "but I reckon there isn't any help for it. Can't take chances of running smack inter a dose of lead pizenin'."

Swearing protests under his bit, Shadow wormed his way through the thorny growth. Finally Slade heard a musical tinkle of water and a moment later they entered a tiny clearing where a little spring bubbled forth a clear| stream. Slade swung down from the saddle.

"Okay, feller," he told Shadow. "You can just hang 'round here for a spell and see what you can do for this grass. Now don't go blasting yore haid off and giving the game away."

Leaving the horse he slipped through the growth on foot, sniffing the smell of burning wood, listening to the complaints of the cattle. As he diagonalled back toward the trail the growth thinned. At a final fringe he halted, peering through the leaves.

Ahead was open space. A little distance up canyon a corral fence had been built and beyond this fence were many cattle. Even at this distance, Slade could see that they bore diversified brands. He gave the scattered herd but a glance, however. In front of him and only a few hundred yards distant was what interested him far more.

It was a small cabin built at the edge of the growth on the far side of the clearing, and from its mud and stick chimney rose a thin column of blue smoke.

With intent eyes Slade studied the cabin. It fronted in his direction, with a window and a door facing the trail. The door was closed, but as he watched, he saw a shadow pass the window.

"Somebody there, all right," he muttered. "Question is, how many somebodies."

He studied the surrounding terrain. "Can slip down the canyon, through the brush, and get in behind the shack," he decided.

He proceeded to do this and a few minutes later found him crouched in the brush directly behind the cabin. There was no window on this side, but there was a back door standing slightly ajar. He couldn't see the inside of the shack, but he could hear voices. He decided there were at least three men inside, perhaps more. He eyed the door longingly, but regretfully shook his black head.

"Too chancy," he muttered. "If I went bustin' in there and a coupla those jiggers happened to be facing this way, and scattered, they'd have a almighty good chance of downing me. But if they were all busy looking the other way—"

For another moment he crouched motionless, the concentration furrow deepening between his black brows. Then he turned and faded into the growth.

"Mebbe it'll work," he mused. "Wuth trying, anyhow. I'm shore I got some rawhide thong in my saddlebags."

He found the thongs—long strips of dry raw-hide—and nodded with satisfaction. Repeatedly he soused one in the water of the spring, kneading and twisting it until it was soaking wet. Then he slid his heavy rifle from the saddle boot and hurried back to his former post in front of the cabin. Here he found a suitable bit of growth and went to work. He bound the rifle firmly to a branch, the muzzle pointing down. Then he bent a second stout branch downward and tied one end of the soaked rawhide thong to it. The other end of the thong he secured to the lower branch. The thong stretched tightly as the upper branch sought to spring back into place. Working swiftly, he tied a second thong, a dry one this time, to the upper branch, made a loop at the other end and slipped it over the trigger of the rifle. There was a little slack in the thong and it hung loosely from the upper branch. But as the tethered branch bore upward, the wet rawhide which secured it slowly stretched, taking up the slack in the cord looped about the trigger. Slade nodded with satisfaction and cocked the rifle.

"Five minutes at the most and she'll be stretched tight enough to shoot the rifle," he decided. "When those hellions in the shack hear a gun bang right out here in front, it's just 'bout certain they'll all herd up to look out the front window. They won't be thinking nothing 'bout the back door. Then we'll see."

He slipped into the growth once more and in a few minutes was crouched behind the cabin. Listening intently, he could hear the men moving about inside. He caught a word or two of the conversation.

"Time we was movin' things. I tell you, Rocky, this deestrict is gettin' hot. Things ain't been right since that big ice-eyed hellion shoved in. It was him stopped the stampede t'other night and drilled Skint's arm. Something almighty funny 'bout that maverick. I've a notion he's aimin' to take over in this deestrict, and if he shoves in some more of his kind, me, I don't want to be here. He—*Good gosh!*"

From directly in front of the cabin, the echo of a booming rifle shot slammed back and forth between the canyon walls. Slade heard the crash of an overturned chair, a thump of boots on the floor, then a clatter of steps toward the front of the cabin. Jerking his guns he streaked for the sagging back door. His shoulder hit it and it flew back with a crash. With a bound Slade was inside the cabin, narrowing his eyes to the change of light.

Slade carefully examined the cabin. Then he went out and gave the gorge a once-over. There were plenty of cattle in the canyon, wearing various Cienaga Valley brands, but he quickly decided that the gorge was not the real hangout of the Shotgun Riders, but merely a hole-in-the-wall holding spot for rustled cattle.

"Looks like I'm no nearer the finish of this pertickler chore than when I rode in here," he mused. "But," he added hopefully, "I 'pear to be thinning out the gang considerable, and that helps. Will send some of the boys here tomorrow to round up these beefs and drive them back where they belong. Reckon Gordon and the other owners won't feel over bad about that."

Running up the left slope of the gorge was a faint trail that he concluded would doubtless afford a short cut back to town. Securing Shadow, he sent the big black up the slope. He had ridden for some miles and was traversing a winding track that hugged a towering wall of stone on one side, with a sheer drop to dark fangs of stone and a gleam of white water fully five hundred feet below.

Suddenly he straightened in the saddle, peering ahead with narrowed eyes.

"Shadow," he exclaimed, "what in blazes kind of a contraption do you suppose that can be? Is some jigger aiming to trap eagles?"

The trail curved here, and from where he rode, the shallow curve, he could glance along the chord of the arc to where, a quarter of a mile distant by the straight line and nearly twice that around the shallow curve, a spur of granite jutted out over the shuddery depths of the canyon which flanked the lip of the trail. To the tip of this spur was suspended a large wooden cage, held in place, so far as Slade could ascertain, by a rope set in a groove cut in the tip of the spur, its hither end being secured to a knob of stone. Hung above the groove was something that flashed in the sunlight.

Through the openings between the wooden bars of the cage, Slade could discern a bulky object.

"Looks like bait of some kind," he mused, "but I don't see a door for anything to get in. Mebbe it's on the far side, though. June along, feller, and let's see what we can make of it."

Shadow quickened his pace, his ears pricked forward, his great liquid eyes apparently fixed on the object which intrigued his tall master.

Slade, lounging carelessly in his high-cantled stock saddle, studied the swinging cage, his entire attention to all appearances, fixed on the singular object; but in truth, his long, black-lashed gray eyes missed no minutest detail of the surrounding landscape. Particularly did he note the irregular and brush clothed rim of the canyon's far wall, a good seven hundred yards distant, with the slanting rays of the westering sun beating fiercely against the dark rock.

"One helluva hole, feller," he told the black horse. "Slip over the edge and you'd get plumb hungry 'fore you hit bottom!"

Shadow snorted agreement, and quickened his pace.

The outlines of the suspended cage grew more distinct as horse and rider swung around the long arc of the trail. The bulky object inside began to take on form. Slade regarded it with increasing interest. Suddenly he straightened in the saddle, his eye narrowing, his bronzed face bleak. The gray eyes lost their sunny light and turned cold as the spray of a frozen waterfall. In an instinctive gesture, his slim right hand dropped toward the black butt of one of the big guns that snugged in carefully oiled and worked cut-out holsters slung low against the wearer's muscular thighs. He spoke, his musical voice abruptly hard and brittle—

"There's a man inside that damn thing, and he's

alive! I can see his hands moving. Trail, Shadow! He's yelling something!"

The great horse shot forward, irons drumming the hard surface of the trail. He stretched his glossy neck, his nostrils flaring redly, and seemed to fairly pour his long body over the ground. His rider leaned forward in the saddle, tense, alert, studying the writhing figure inside the cage.

"Tied hand and foot!" he suddenly exclaimed. "Can't do more than wiggle about. Now what in blazes—"

The speculating voice snapped off, sounded again in a single horror-reeking curse. Face whitening, Slade leaned still farther forward in the saddle as the great black horse raced around the curve.

The queer cage was no longer in sight. Without the slightest warning it had plummeted into the depths, tumbling crazily as the weight within it shifted. Up from the grim canyon knifed a wailing cry that swiftly threaded to a thin agony of sound. There was a distant glassy crashing, then silence.

Slade straightened in the saddle, and with an iron grip pulled Shadow to a foaming halt where the granite spur jutted forth from the parent rock of the cliff. Wordless, he sat staring at the grooved spur, and at the still smoldering end of the thin grass rope that had whipped back almost to the trail as the strain upon it was so abruptly relieved.

Bewildered, for the moment uncomprehending, The Hawk stared at the charred rope end. Then his gaze shifted upward, to the gleaming object which hung above the spur tip. He swore between set teeth as he abruptly understood the nature of the devilish contrivance.

The gleaming object was only a very ordinary whiskey bottle filled with water and suspended from a cleft stick whose butt end was jammed into a crevice in the rock.

"But the damndest, cold-bloodedest contraption for murder any hellion ever figgered out," he told the black horse. "See how it works: the bottle filled with water hung so that when the sun reaches a certain point in the sky, the rays pass through the water in the bottle just like through a burning glass, and focus on the rope where it passes through the groove. The dry grass fibres catch on fire pronto and burn till the rope gets so weak it can't bear the weight of the cage. Then she breaks and the cage drops to the canyon floor. And that pore devil, tied hand and foot, hadda lie in there and watch the sun ray creep nearer and nearer to the rope until it reached it! Of all the hellish things!"

Swiftly his glance traveled about. "Trail not traveled over much," he muttered, "practically no chance of anybody coming along and turning him loose. No wonder he squirmed and yelled when he heard yore irons on the trail, feller! If we'd just been a minute sooner! We'd—*Trail!*"

Shadow set forward in a surging bound. At the same instant Slade went sideways out of the saddle, struck the earth on racing feet, hand gripping the bit ring, and swerved the black horse into the half-light at the base of the overhanging cliff, where he was almost invisible against the dark stone.

Whe-e-e-e—cra-a-a-ck! Wham!

Something yelled through the air and slammed against the cliff face with a metallic thudding sound. Again it came, flicking dust from the stone, showering horse and man with stinging rock fragments. Shadow snorted nervously, shivered, but otherwise stood motionless as a horse sculptured from black marble. Shadow had been under fire before and knew how to obey orders without question.

With a deft, effortless motion, Slade whipped the heavy Winchester from where it snugged in the saddle boot. He crouched beside his rigid mount, tense, alert, every sense keyed to the highest pitch. His gray eyes searched the distant canyon rim for another glimpse of the tiny gleam of shifting metal that had warned him just in time.

Abruptly the rifle flung up, the butt clamped against *El Halcon*'s shoulder, his bronzed cheek nestled against the stock. For an instant the cold eyes glanced along the sights; then the rifle spoke.

Far across the dark gulf, where an overhang of brush clothed the ragged rim, a puff of dust jumped into being. It was instantly followed by a grayish smoke smear barely showing against the green of the foliage. A third slug yelled through the air and smacked against the cliff face a scant yard from the crouching Hawk. For a tense instant he held his fire; then, as once more the tell-tale gleam of sunlight on shifting metal disclosed the presence of the unseen drygulcher, the Winchester boomed sullenly.

This time there was answering movement in the growth across the canyon—a wild waving of branches, a bunching of shadows.

His lean hawk-face set like granite, his gray eyes cold, *El Halcon* watched a writhing figure pitch from amid the growth, clear the ragged canyon lip and rush downward, turning over and over, limbs sprawling grotesquely in the air. Amid the tangled brush and black stone fangs jutting up from the canyon floor it vanished. The sunlight gleamed for a flickering breath on the falling rifle which accompanied it. Then the growth and the canyon rim were again devoid of motion.

Chapter 14

For long minutes Slade crouched motionless, eyes searching the growth, rifle ready. Finally he straightened up, deliberately stepped out onto the sun drenched lip of the trail, poised there for a fleeting instant, and zigzagged back into the shadow.

No answering whine of lead or glinting gleam of metal attended the move. Again he crouched, combing the ragged lip with a glance that missed not the smallest detail. Then he straightened up, fumbled a collapsible rod and a swab from a saddle pocket and deftly cleaned the rifle. He refilled the magazine, slipped the Winchester back into the boot and nodded to Shadow.

"Reception c'mittee of one, I reckon," he remarked, adding grimly, "and his twine is coiled for him all proper."

Fearlessly, he walked out onto the narrow granite spur, poised on the thin tip and leaned over the awful depths beneath. Amid the rock five hundred feet below he could make out the shattered fragments of the cage. And that bulkier blotch half hidden by a straggle of bush must be all remaining of the hapless prisoner.

Slade shook his black head, and glanced across the canyon, marking well the spot where the hidden drygulcher had hurtled to death. He gazed long and earnestly down the canyon, the mouth of which was somewhere beyond the jutting shoulder of the cliff. He noted, however, that the gorge widened and the far rim lowered swiftly as it curved.

"Which figgers that the mouth hadn't oughta be so over far off," he reasoned aloud. "Shadow, we'll just nacherly go see, pertickler as we're headed in the gen'ral direction anyhow. Mebbe we can slip back up the gulley before come dark. Those two jiggers might have something valuable in their pockets."

Shadow nodded his head sagely. Slade swung into the hull and rode swiftly down the trail, his eyes still searching every foot of the distant canyon rim.

The trail swung around the arc, curved about the cliff shoulder and straightened out. Another two miles of curves and tangents and Slade nodded with satisfaction. A mile ahead was the canyon mouth, with the gray ribbon of the trail rolling down a sharp slope and swerving past its dark portals less than a thousand yards to the east of them.

The cliffs on Slade's left were lowering, as was the long slant of the mountains above them. They plunged away to a crumbling slope as he reached a point where the trail swerved sharply southeast in the direction of Cienaga.

Slade left the trail and turned into the rocky, brush-choked canyon, with a swift stream purling along the far wall.

He found the shattered cage after considerable searching; nearby was the mangled victim. Every bone in the man's body apeared to be broken. But, strangely, the face was not particularly marred.

Slade gazed into the haggard, tortured countenance. It was not a pleasant face. The complexion was swarthy, the hair lank and black. The mouth a thin gash in the marred face.

"Salty looking jigger," he muttered. "Wonder why in blazes was a thing like this done to him?"

The man's pockets proved to be empty. The shattered cage offered little of interest. It was roughly constructed of short lengths of saplings bound together with strips of rawhide. The fragment of grass rope by which it had been suspended had apparently once been part of a lariat.

Then abruptly he saw something wedged amid the wreckage of the cage. It was a sawed-off shotgun, broken in two at the smallest part of the stock.

Slade stared at the shattered weapon, perplexity in his eyes. Then suddenly the concentration furrow deepened between his black brows.

"Looks like it had been deliberately broken across," he muttered. "Like an officer's sword when he's kicked out of the service for misconduct or failure to perform his duty. Blazes! I believe that's it! Uh-huh, I'll bet a hatful of pesos that's the explanation. This hellion was one of the Shotgun Riders. He failed up some way or other, and this was their nice little way of doing him in. Bust his shotgun across and cash him in this way as a warning to others. Nice outfit, all right, and one with brains at the head, and imagination. Reckon it'll be quite a spell before one of the gang slips again. And I've a plumb notion, this jigger was the leader of that raid on Gordon's herd last night. The price of failure! Reign by terror—that's allus the way with this kind of an outfit. Only this one is tops. Shooting a jigger through the head doesn't make over much of an impression on salty gents; but hanging him up in a cage like that to wait and wait until the sun burns the rope through and lets him fall is some-thing else again. They even set a lookout to see that nobody meddled with the contraption and let the jigger loose before it fell."

Thoughtfully, he stared across the canyon toward the south wall, where a cleft in the cliff marked the fall of the drygulcher.

"Body had oughta be lying right under that crack," he mused. His glance shifted to the lowering sky.

"Reckon we got time to slide across there 'fore the storm breaks," he told Shadow. "We're gonna get soaked 'fore we can make it to town, anyhow."

The distance across the canyon was not great, but the going was so rough, with entangling brush, half concealed boulders and wicked fangs of stone, that it took much longer to reach the far wall than Slade had anticipated. And as he broke through a final fringe of thicket, near the flank of a huge chimney rock, he realized that he had made the difficult crossing for nothing.

The crack, the gleam of which he had caught a glimpse of earlier in the evening, washed the south wall of the gorge, and the water ran swift and deep. Slade glowered at the dark, hurrying surface.

"That hellion pitched right into the crik when he landed," he grumbled. "The current woulda grabbed him and carried him a long way down stream pronto. Nope, no use looking for him around here, even if it was still light enough to see anything under those bushes, which it isn't. And here comes that sockdollager of a storm in another five minutes. Shadow, looks to me like we'll hafta hole up here for a spell; never could make back across to the trail in the dark and the rain. Mebbe we can find an overhang or something on the other side of this chimney rock. Plenty of grass and water here for you, and there's wood to make a fire, and I got a few scraps of chuck in my saddlebags."

He guided the black around the ragged angle

of the chimney rock, and a moment later exclaimed with satisfaction.

The chimney rock proved to be a regular Devil's Kitchen of upward flinging spires, and at the broad base of one was a deep hollow protected by an overhang of stone. It was in reality a shallow cave and promised ample shelter from the storm.

Swiftly The Hawk got the rig off Shadow and turned him loose to water and graze, knowing that the well trained cayuse would not stray and would come seeking shelter when the storm got bad. Then he gathered dry wood, of which there was plenty in the thickets, got a fire going and made himself comfortable. Before the rain arrived with a howl of wind, blazing lightning and crackling thunder, coffee was boiling in a little flat bucket, bacon was sizzling in a small skillet and a doughcake was ready to fry in the fat.

Shadow sidled to the shelter of the overhang a little later, still munching a mouthful of succulent gramma grass. Slade waved a welcoming hand and helped himself to another cake and more steaming coffee. Finally, with a deep sigh of satisfaction, he settled his back against the rocky wall and soaked in the agreeable heat from the fire as he contemplated the sheets of water beating down in front of his snug shelter. Over the blue trickle of his cigarette, he gravely addressed the black horse.

"There's us'ly reasons for a killing like we saw done by way of that damned cage, feller," he announced. "And I'm sure for certain we guessed right the very first time. Uh-huh, looks like we're in for quite a nice time in this section."

He smoked thoughtfully for a few minutes longer, then pinched out the butt of his brain tablet and cast it aside. Chuckling to himself, he drummed softly with his fingers, as on imaginary guitar strings. Then he flung back his black head, and a moment later the rocky walls of the cave echoed back the music of a rich voice singing a rollicking old song of the range:

> Button up yore slicker,
> Cowboy, and ride,
> For there never was a rain
> What could wet a hoss inside!

Outside the thunder boomed and rolled. The wind howled and whimpered around the weird pinnacles of the chimney rocks. The level lances of the rain hissed down, golden in the leaping glow of Slade's fire, pale silver in the blue glare of the lightning. It was a wild night, with little of comfort of peace to mark its passing.

But snugly sheltered by the cave, and warmed by the fire, *El Halcon* sang on in his unbelievably sweet and powerful voice, his gay songs of the range, his haunting melodies of the mountains

160

and the wastelands, his sweet and wistful love songs of Old Spain.

The storm ceased as suddenly as it began. The roll of thunder died to a mutter that lost itself beyond the eastern rim of the world. The roar of the wind became a weary whisper, softened to a drowsy sigh. The hurrying clouds curled up like torn paper and the mellow light of a full moon streamed into the canyon.

Walt Slade stood up, stretched his long arms until they almost touched the roof of the cave.

"Reckon we might as well june on to town while we can, feller," he told Shadow.

The boulders and the wet brush took on strange and deceptive shapes in the moonlight, but Shadow picked his way daintily across the rough canyon floor on sure hoofs and reached the far wall without mishap. Upon reaching the semblance of a trail, Slade gave him his head and rode town-ward at a swift gait.

The dawn was breaking in rose and scarlet and glowing gold when they reached Cienaga. Slade, after seeing to it that all of Shadow's wants were provided for, went to bed in the little room above the stalls of Bart Coster's livery stable and slept soundly until early afternoon.

After eating, Slade decided to ride back to the ranch. He rode carelessly and at ease, thinking hard on the happenings of the night before. Overhead the clouds gathered, and as he entered the hills, the dark of evening was already beginning to sift down in mystic purple from their heights.

"Looks like that darn storm of last night is headed back this way," The Hawk muttered, glancing at the lowering sky. "June along, boss, before you grow fins and web-toes."

Heedless of the gathering storm, *El Halcon* rode on toward his first real contact and his most weird experience with the mad genius who headed the dread Shotgun Riders.

Chapter 15

The trail wound on silent and deserted, gray and shadowy under the overcast sky. The dark growth overhung it unruffled by movement, the silence broken only by the wind that sighed sadly through the leaves.

Rain began to fall, first with a fine mist, then a slow, steady downpour that beat on the growth with a low mutter that drowned the sighing of the chill wind. Slade unstrapped his slicker and buttoned it tight. Shadow snorted disgustedly and shivered the clinging drops from his glossy coat.

Suddenly the black's ears pricked forward. Instantly Slade was alert. He had heard nothing, but Shadow undoubtedly had. Slade glanced across the canyon, back to the trail swathed in the shifting rain veil. He dropped his hand to the butt of the Winchester snugged in the boot and keenly eyed the bend a few hundred yards ahead. He bent his head as he did so to avoid a low hanging that protruded over the trail. He heard a snaky whisper overhead and flung erect an instant too late.

Something hissed through the air from the concealing growth. A tight loop dropped over The Hawk's head and shoulder and was instantly jerked taut, pinning his arms to his sides. With a convulsive movement he managed to half draw the Winchester, then he was hurled from the saddle to crash on the wet ground with stunning force. The rope whipped a second turn about him as he struggled half erect and jerked him down again. There was a crash in the growth and two men plunged into the trail. Slade had a glimpse of dark, beastly faces framed in lank black hair. Then a gun barrel crashed against his head and he went limp.

A dark hand reached for Shadow's bridle. The owner recoiled with a scream of pain as gleaming teeth slashed his arm from elbow to wrist. There was a clatter of hoofs and Shadow flashed into the rain mists and vanished. The bitten man cursed in a queer stuttering jargon and sent a vengeful bullet after the fleeing horse.

"Cut that damn nonsense," barked a gruff voice from the growth. "Tie that hellion's hands and fasten a handkerchief over his eyes. He'll come outa it in a minute. Load him onto Juan's hoss and tie his legs to the stirrup straps. Yuh'll hafta ride behind him, Juan, and hold him in the hull till he gets his senses back. Get a move on!"

Dimly Slade realized he was being lifted to a horses's back by men who grunted with the strain. His hands were tied behind him, a blindfold was bound over his eyes. He sagged forward until his face was buried in the cayuse's coarse mane. His senses were coming back, but he was still dazed from the blow on his head and his muscles felt like water.

The horse got under way. For a mile or more they followed the trail, then turned from it and he descended a steep slope. Slade felt the slap and pull of wet branches against his legs and knew that the horse was forcing its way through thick growth. Direction changed continually and although he tried hard to map the course in his mind, he soon became utterly confused.

"Just the same I bet a peso ol' Shadow is follering on my tail," he muttered to himself.

Soon the course leveled off. Slade could no longer feel the touch of foliage. The horse's irons echoed back from a nearby wall or slope, the speed increased. Slade was fully conscious now and his strength was returning. However, he continued to sag over his mount's neck and simulate utter helplessness.

The trail his captors were evidently following wound on. The echoes ceased and The Hawk gathered that the track had either edged away from the slope or a gorge they had been traversing had widened. The horses were travelling at a good clip now and had undoubtedly covered a considerable distance since leaving the trail.

Some light had seeped through the bandage that covered his eyes at first, but this gradually dimmed and ceased.

"Must be getting dark," he told himself.

Another half hour or so passed. Slade's strained position, leaning forward in the saddle as he was, began to numb his body and at length he decided that nothing was to be gained by further decep-tion. Bound as he was, he was helpless, and his captors were doubtless on the alert. He groaned, writhed, shook his head and struggled against his bonds in the bewildered way of a man just regaining consciousness. Finally he lifted him-self erect, swaying and jerking in the saddle.

"Take it easy," a gruff voice growled. "Sit steady and behave yoreself or yuh'll get another clout 'longside the haid."

"What happened?" The Hawk mumbled uncertainly.

"Never yuh mind what happened—yuh'll find out soon enough," the voice replied. "Set tight and shet up."

Slade obeyed. Another ten minutes and the horse was jerked to a halt. A moment later he felt his legs freed from the stirrup straps.

"All right, tumble off," the voice ordered.

Awkwardly, because of his bound hands, The Hawk managed to slide to the ground. A rough hand seized him and propelled him forward. He stumbled ahead, halted when told to do so, and heard a door open. Again he was shoved forward, felt smooth boards under his feet and heard the door close behind him. The lashings

166

were undone, he was shoved into a chair and the blindfold removed.

At first his eyes were dazzled by the flame of a bracket lamp set high on the wall, then, as his vision cleared, he stared at the man seated on the opposite side of the table, whose face was masked, and who Slade quickly decided was the mysterious Chief of the Shotgun Riders.

For a long moment the Chief met his gaze in silence. Then he spoke, in harsh, gutteral tones.

"Reckon yuh're wonderin' why I had yuh brought here 'stead of havin' the boys do yuh in fust off?" he said.

"Surprised me some," Slade admitted.

The Chief nodded slowly, and did not reply at once.

"I got somethin' special arranged for you," he said at length. "Uh-huh, somethin' plumb special. Yuh did in three of my men yest'day. Not that that matters over much. There's plenty more where they come from; but doin' me outa that herd is somethin' else again."

He ceased speaking, and again bent his glittering glare on The Hawk's face, his eyes smokily dark through the holes of his mask.

"Yuh look sorta shaky and not up to par," he remarked unexpectedly. He raised his voice and spoke to a man who evidently stood behind Slade.

"Get this feller some coffee and chuck," he ordered. "I reckon he sorta needs both."

Steps sounded and, a moment later, the rattle of crockery and cooking utensils. Shortly a plate of food and a large mug of steaming coffee were set before Slade.

"Get on the outside of that and yuh'll feel better," the Chief counselled.

The whole business seemed preposterous, under the circumstances, but Slade was thankful for both food and drink and did not pause to argue the question. He fell to it with a will and felt his strength returning with every mouthful.

As he ate, he glanced around the room, which was of good size, evidently the main room of a large and well built log cabin. A double tier of bunks were built along the opposite wall, on one of which lounged two of the savage looking Seri Indians, hands close to their guns, their beady eyes taking in his every move. To his right was a door secured by a ponderous iron bolt which passed under a hasp driven into the logs. There was a square opening in the upper half of the door. This opening was barred with iron. A second closed door, evidently leading to the outside, pierced the opposite end wall of the cabin and was also bolted.

"Yeah, I brought yuh to this hangout for two pertickler reasons," the Chief remarked, as Slade shoved aside his empty plate and reached for the makin's. He waited until *El Halcon* had got his smoke going, and then spoke again.

168

"Uh-huh, for two pertickler reasons," he repeated. "One of 'em is I don't like a feller what's done me a bad turn to die over fast or easy. We'll take that up later. The other one is 'cause I've heerd yuh play the gitter and sing sorta nice. I like good music and hanker for it ev'ry now and then."

As Slade stared at him in astonishment, he rose to his feet and crossed the room with a gliding stride that reminded Slade of the stalk of a hunting wolf. He slid back the bolt of the inner door and flung it open.

Rusty hinges screamed shrill protest as the door swung back. Slade caught a glimpse of a bunk built against the far wall of the inner room before the Chief obscured it with his bulk.

The bandit leader vanished into the shadowy interior and Slade could hear him rummaging about. A moment later he reappeared, carrying in his hand a guitar.

"Hadda plug a Mexican to get it," he remarked, "but she looks like a purty good one."

He shoved the instrument across the table to Slade, and sat down.

"When yuh've finished that brain tablet, yuh can play and sing for me," he announced. "If yuh can do it as good as I've been told, mebbe yuh won't die so soon as I'd figgered."

Through the smoke of his cigarette, Slade regarded the tall outlaw, and he quickly arrived at a conclusion. This merciless killer was a madman, of that he had not the last doubt. Madness burned in the deepset, glittering eyes.

The outlaw seemed to read menace in the Hawk's steady gaze, for suddenly he gloomed at Slade.

"Don't try nothin' funny," he warned harshly. "Bart has got yore guns and he's settin' right behind yuh with one of 'em p'inted at yore back. I know yuh're plumb salty, and I've heard how yuh've done in a lot of fellers and skimmed the cream off the good things they'd worked up; but yuh fooled yoreself when yuh horned in on my game. All right, let's have a little music."

Slade pinched out the butt of his cigarette, picked up the guitar and tuned it. He ran his slim, bronzed fingers over the strings with crisp power. Then he sang, and as the great 'golden' metallic baritone-bass pealed and thundered in the closed room, the Chief sat entranced. Outside the wind shrieked and moaned. The rain lashed the panes of the barred window and pattered on the roof. The Seri Indians crouched on the bunk like brooding demons, grotesque and unreal in the dim flare of the smoking lamp. And *El Halcon*, a mocking light in his gray eyes, sang on in the gray shadow of death.

Chapter 16

Something of the storm that shook the cabin was in that song. And something of the crash of white water on the rocks. And something of the murmur of soft rain and the rustling of the first green leaves of spring. And something, too, of the calm courage that dares to seek out evil in its strongest fortress and give winning battle in the face of overwhelming odds.

Finally, after a long time, Slade laid the guitar on the table and began rolling another cigarette. The Chief started, as does a man who comes suddenly out of a dream. His glittering eyes fixed on Slade's face.

"Yeah, yuh got everythin' they said yuh had," he rumbled. "Guess I won't cash yuh in t'night after all—not before t'morrow, anyhow. I might get a hankerin' for a mite more of music, and mebbe I won't. There's a bunk in that other room—yuh can sleep in there t'night. The door's bolted solid and the winder's barred, and Bart and Juan will be sleepin' out here, so it ain't any use for yuh to try anythin' funny. Get in there."

He stood up, gigantic in the dim light, and gestured toward the open door. Slade nodded, picked up the guitar and sauntered leisurely across the room. The door swung shut on its screaming hinges, the Chief shot the bolt which slid into place noiselessly. Slade leaned the guitar against the wall and sat down on the bunk. Through the opening he could see the Chief and the lanky Bart moving about.

"Sounds like the rain's stopped, and I reckon the moon had oughta be out soon," he heard the Chief rumble. "Yuh come with me, Felipe, it's time we was movin'. Bart, I'm leavin' you and Juan to keep cases on that feller. If yuh let him wiggle outa the loop while I'm gone—well, yuh know me!"

A moment later his heavy steps crossed the room to the outer door, one of the lean Seris gliding after him. The door opened, banged shut. A little later Slade heard hoofbeats move away from the cabin. He pinched out his cigarette and stretched his long body on the bunk. Staring at the heavy ceiling boards, dimly visible in the bar of light that streamed through the opening, he pondered his chances of getting out of about the toughest spot he had ever been in.

For a long time The Hawk lay motionless on the smelly bunk. He could hear the occupants of the outer room moving about and occasionally the opening was shadowed as one or the other peered through at their silent prisoner. Gradually the sounds ceased, and the mutter of conversation. A bunk creaked as a heavy body stretched out on it, then another. Silence broken only by the sound of a restless turning or twisting descended inside the cabin. The moan of the wind seemed louder in contrast, but the raindrops no longer spattered the window panes.

Still *El Halcon* lay quietly on his bunk. Finally a new sound broke the silence, a discordant but rhythmic sound varied only by an occasional snort. Slade strained his ears to listen. At length, he was convinced that two men snored in the outer room. He sat up, swung his legs over the edge of the bunk, listened a moment and then glided across the room on noiseless feet. Standing well back in the shadow, he peered through the opening. He could just make out the forms of his guards occupying two of the double tier of bunks that lined the side wall. The guttering lamp also showed his guns lying on the table, far beyond his reach. He studied the scene for a moment, then turned to the single window of the inner room.

A glance sufficed to convince him that it offered no avenue of escape. It was narrow, and crisscrossed with heavy iron bars set solidly in the logs. He turned back to the door opening, approached it softly and peered through. He could see the knobbed end of the ponderous bolt, which was beyond arm's reach. He surveyed it with a calculating eye. Then he softly lifted the guitar from where it leaned against the wall and began unwinding one of the steel strings. It was not by chance that he had carried the guitar with him when he entered his prison.

It took but a few minutes to loosen the string and detach it from the instrument. He deftly fashioned a sliding loop in one end, and again studied the bolt which secured the door.

"I can lasso it, all right, but the angle will be so sharp I can't pull it from under the hasp," he muttered under his breath.

He turned back and removed a second string from the guitar. This he fastened securely to the first wire a couple of inches above the loop. Then he carefully thrust the noosed end through the opening and patiently fished for the knob. After what seemed an eternity of nervous effort, he finally managed to slip the noose over the bolt end and draw it tight. Then he secured the upper end of the string to the bar which blocked the opening. He slid the upper end of the second string to the corner of the opening farthest from the bolt and gently drew it taut. He jiggled the string, tightening and releasing it, careful to make not the slightest sound.

The bolt slipped slightly, caught, resisted his efforts. Patiently he worked the string back and forth, putting on the pressure with tiny jerks.

The bolt creaked, then shot back with a sharp click. Slade stood utterly motionless, straining his ears and eyes for sound or movement from the bunks. The snoring continued uninterrupted.

With a sigh of relief he relaxed, and considered the situation.

He recalled the screaming hinges of the door and knew he could not hope to open it without arousing the sleepers. His only chance was to fling the door open with abrupt suddenness, dash across the room and secure his guns before the two guards were fully aware what was going on.

And there was another contingency upon which his chances hinged. He wondered with painful intensity whether Bart had unloaded the guns before placing them on the table. There was a good chance that he had done so: men familiar with weapons do not make a practice of leaving them lying around loaded. If the guns were empty, the cards were perilously stacked against him. But it was a desperate chance he had to take. He could see that both Bart and the Seri were sleeping with their Colts strapped to their waists, and he knew that men of their calibre usually slept like dogs, with one eye open, and came awake in full possession of their faculties.

His cartridge belts had not been removed. He loosened several brass shells in the loops, drawing them almost free. Then, with a final glance at the sleepers, he flung the door wide open and went across the room in a streaking bound. He had the long-barrelled sixes in his hands before the door banged against the wall.

A single glance realized his worst fears. *The*

cartridges had been removed from the chambers!

The snaky Seri was already out of his bunk and on his feet, hand streaking to his gun. Moving with racing speed, Slade jerked a cartridge from its sloop, shoved it into the cylinder, spun the chamber into line with the barrel and fired point-blank. The Seri's gun exploded even as he slammed backward as from the blow of a mighty fist. But the shock of the heavy slug tearing through his breast threw him off balance a split second before he pulled trigger, and his bullet went wild. Slade hurled himself sideways and down as Bart shot from the hip. He had a second cartridge out of the loop and into the cylinder before the outlaw could line sights a second time.

The two guns blazed together. With a strangled cry, Bart sank back into his blankets, twitched and was still. But Walt Slade, blood pouring down his face, tried to raise himself to his knees on arms that crumpled under him, and then fell forward on his face to lie as motionless as the two dead outlaws, while the great clock of the sky wheeled westward and the first streamers of the dawn reddened the tops of the mountains.

Chapter 17

Full morning had not broken when Walt Slade raised his bloody face from the floor and glared wildly about. His glance fell on the graying window panes.

He retrieved his fallen guns, clumsily fumbled cartridges from his bolt and loaded them. Then he holstered the Colts and raised trembling fingers to the bloody furrow that creased his scalp just above the hairline. Clutching at the table for support, he staggered to his feet and stood swaying.

The room was a blood spattered shambles. The corpse of Bart lay huddled in his sodden blankets. The Seri was slumped against the lower bunk, his dead eyes staring stonily. The cabin was deathly still.

Getting a grip on himself, Slade stumbled to the stove, poured a cup of still warm coffee and swallowed it at a gulp. As he replaced the cup, a shelf above the stove caught his eye. It was lined with irregular fragments of broken rock. Automatically he plucked one from its resting place and stared at it dazedly. Shaking his head in a bewildered way, he fumbled the bit of stone into his pockets. Then he picked up his hat from where it lay on one of the bunks and gingerly placed it on his wounded head.

"Gotta get outa this before some other hellions get here," he mumbled. "Now if ol' Shadow just hasn't failed up!"

He unbolted the door and slipped out, breathing great gulps of the clean morning air and feeling his swimming head clear as he did so. He pursed his lips and whistled a clear, musical note. Almost instantly a plaintive whinny answered from amid the growth which flanked the cabin on all sides. There was a soft patter of hoofs and Shadow ambled out of the brush, his ears pricked for-ward, his great liquid eyes peering inquiringly. He thrust his velvety muzzle into Slade's hand and blew a snorting breath. Slade patted the sleek, black neck, gathered up the trailing reins and clumsily mounted.

A trail wound through the growth from in front of the cabin. Slade let the reins fall on Shadow's neck and spoke to him. The black horse unhesitatingly headed along the trail.

"That's the way you come to get here, all right," The Hawk muttered. "It's up to you to find the way out, oldtimer."

Shadow snorted and quickened his pace. Slade let the reins hang limp and strained his ears for the sound of approaching horsemen.

The light had strengthened and he could see

that he was in a fairly wide canyon densely grown with tall brush and occasional trees. The trail, a mere trace, wound through the growth and a glance told Slade it had been traveled since the rain began the afternoon before.

The walls of the canyon were lofty and almost sheer. The brush was so thick that he could see but a few dozen yards at most along the winding trail. His faculties knew he would have but scant chance should he encounter the Chief and his men along the narrow track.

It was with a feeling of decided relief that he reached the point where the canyon opened onto the rangeland and he began to get his bearings.

"Wonder how many of those squats they have, anyhow," he muttered. "Seems the hills are full of 'em and they can hole up anywhere they take a notion."

He was convinced that the cabin was not the real rendezvous of the Shotgun Riders. It had all the earmarks of a shack built years before by some wandering hunter or prospector and appropriated by the gang for convenient temporary quarters.

"Smart hellion in lots of ways," he mused, apropos of the tall Chief. "Keeps his real hangout under cover all the time. Got Seri Indians in his outfit, too. They're the smartest trackers in the Southwest, and the chances are they know these hills like they know the palms of their hands. Which comes in mighty handy for a jigger in his line of business."

In the course of his experience, he had garnered other valuable information. He had quickly arrived at the conclusion that the Mysterious Chief was decidedly other than that which he tried to make out to be. His speech had been an absurd parody of Southwest dialect, and his mannerisms had also been forced and unnatural, which had not passed unnoted by the observant Hawk. Then there was his taste for good music.

Slade had purposefully picked his songs with care, refraining from the crude doggerels, the homely ditties and uncouth hoe-down so popular with the illiterate plainsman. And the Chief had asked for none of these, but had sat entranced and appreciative.

"A man used to the better things of life, an educated man with educated tastes," Slade mused as he rode homeward. "Plumb out of place, and doubly dangerous as a consequence. Uh-huh, looks like I sure got my work cut out for me. Luck to get out of this shindig tonight with nothing worse than a skinned head. Well, I sure am thinning the gang out, anyhow."

After reaching the ranch, Slade attended to his head injury, which, as he had surmised, proved slight. Later in the afternoon he rode to the construction camp. He was playing a hunch and was greatly pleased at the first manifestation of its working.

There was nobody in the office but Taylor's clerk, an amiable youth who was undoubtedly bored with the routine.

"Mr. Allison is in Cienaga, contracting for supplies," said the boy. "Mr. Taylor is down at the lower yard."

"I'm anxious to see Taylor," Slade told him. "Think you could round him up?"

"Certainly, sir, I'll be glad to tell him, if you'll stay in the office till I get back," the clerk replied with alacrity, plainly glad of a chance to get into the air for even a brief space.

"Plumb nice of you," the Hawk drawled. "Sure I'll stick around till you get back."

The boy departed, whistling. Slade watched him dawdle down the yard. He knew that a clear half hour would elapse before the clerk returned, with or without Taylor. Closing the outer door, and shooting the bolt, he went to work with efficiency.

Allison, the assistant, he had learned used the inner office and kept his data there. Slade glanced at the papers on the desk, absorbing their contents but finding nothing of interest. Next he tackled the desk drawers. The second from the top was locked; but the top drawer was not. The Hawk grinned slightly as he removed the top drawer from its slides. As was customary with this type of desk, the bottom of the top drawer formed the top of the one below it.

"They allus slip up on the little things," he chuckled to himself.

He thrust a hand through the opening and began drawing forth the contents of the locked drawer. There were papers and pamphlets dealing with abstruse engineering problems, some written in English, others in German or French. The concentration furrow was deep between Slade's brows and his strangely colored eyes were glowing as he glanced through the collection, some of which he could decipher, others of which he could not. He drew forth a small black book and read the presentation inscription, shaking his head as he did so.

"Ph. D.," he murmured aloud, "Doctor of Philosophy!" He stared at the mute evidence that the owner of the volume boasted the highest scholastic degree a famous University could confer.

Gently, almost reverently, he laid the book aside and drew forth something that had been carefully stowed in a far corner of the drawer. It was a circular briquet, dull black in color, quite heavy. It dimpled slightly to the warm pressure of a forefinger. Slade stared at it, the concentration furrow deepening still more. He turned it over in his bronzed fingers, "hefted" it in his palm, sniffed the heavy, oily odor it gave off.

Then with great care he replaced it exactly where he had found it. He likewise replaced the other articles he had taken from the drawer so that only the most meticulous examination of the contents would show that they had been disturbed. Then he slipped the upper drawer into place and gave the desk a final careful scrutiny. He was sitting in the outer office, thoughtfully smoking a cigarette, when Duncan Taylor arrived.

Had Taylor not been so absorbed with his own problems at the moment, he might have felt that the matter about which Slade wished to consult him, pertaining to the size and date of delivery of the next trail herd, was not nearly so urgent as he had been led to believe. As it was, he agreed, almost absentmindedly, with the Ranger's suggestions, and then launched into a diatribe against the difficulties of building railroad in this particular "last-end-of-creation."

Slade listened gravely, with sympathetic interest. "I don't see why you don't turn over a lot of that work to yore assistant, Mr. Allison," he suggested mildly when Taylor paused for a breath.

"That's impossible," the engineer rapped impatiently. "Allison is a good man and a hard worker, but he is not a finished engineer. He has neither the requisite knowledge nor the experience necessary to solve such problems as I am speaking of. I can depend on him for routine field work and such, but that is about the limit of his capabilities."

Slade nodded, but said nothing. He was thinking of a little black book.

"It's a heavy burden," complained Taylor. "Too much for one man."

"Perhaps Mr. Dunn, the General Manager, will be on the ground before long," Slade anticipated hopefully, "then you can consult with him."

"I wired an urgent message to the main offices," Taylor said. "They replied that Mr. Dunn was expected to sail shortly and should be out here before much longer. I certainly wish he would hurry up."

Tentatively, Slade voiced a suggestion. "Don't you think it might even now be better to change to the Tonto Pass route instead of fighting the Quag?" he asked persuasively.

Duncan Taylor's stubborn jaw jutted forward. "No," he shot out with decision. "The filling is going to be expensive but not more so than the grading up to and through the Tonto Pass would be, and when we do get this route established, we'll have a splendid grade and roadbed, which is more than we would have by way of the pass. No, Cienaga Valley is the logical route. The road goes through."

Slade said no more. A little later he bade Taylor good-bye and headed for town. He found Keith

Gordon in his office. Gordon handed him a sealed envelope.

"Your answer to that telegram you had me send to the Drovers' Exchange Bank in Dallas," he explained.

Slade tore the envelope and read the single line the message contained. Without comment, but with his black brows drawn together, he handed the paper to Gordon. The saloon keeper stared, his pale eyes widening. He looked up with a bewildered face.

"But I don't understand!" he exclaimed. "What does it mean, and what are you driving at, Slade?"

"I don't know for sure yet," the Hawk admitted frankly, "but I do know that something is going on in this section that won't stand investigation."

Gordon's face set with decision. "The county commissioners have appointed Clate Shaw sheriff to fill out Hank Bevins' term," he said. "I'm going down and have a talk with Shaw, right away. This time I'll give him something to think about."

He turned to go, but Slade put forth a restraining hand.

"Wait," he counseled, "you're going off half-cocked. I don't want any move made yet. Wait until I give you the word."

Gordon stared at his foreman. He had a vague feeling that the status of employer and employee were somehow becoming badly scrambled. In

185

some manner which he could not quite fathom, this tall gray-eyed cowboy had usurped all the authority in sight. But despite his doubts, and his justifiable irritation, he succumbed to a stronger will.

"All right," he grumbled, "I suppose you know what you are doing, but I don't like to be kept in the dark this way."

"Be patient a little while, and mebbe I can give you some light," the Ranger replied earnestly. "I've stumbled on to some queer things in this section, Gordon, things that may strongly affect you and your friends, and, after all, I'm working for you and have yore int'rests at heart. I don't know what all is going on, so I don't want to go making guesses out loud or saying things I may not be able to back with facts. You just hang on and give me the rope I need and mebbe things will work out."

Keith Gordon stared up into the stern bronzed face and level gray eyes, and appeared satisfied with what he read there.

"It sounds loco to me," he declared, "but I've got faith in you, Slade, and I feel that you know what you are about. And, as I mentioned once before, you saved my life, and the life of Doc Groves, one of my oldest and most valued friends. I'm backing your play, no matter what it is. And after the Black Quag finishes off Taylor and his railroad building and Wade Thorne takes over my spread and business, I'll trail along with you when you go looking for a new job," he added disgustedly.

Slade grinned down at him, and patted him on the shoulder.

"I've a hunch it isn't going to be as bad as all that," he consoled. "Well, I've got to hustle back to the spread and see how the boys are coming along with that herd."

Slade was not grinning, however, as he rode the trail to Cienaga Valley. His face was bleak, his eyes somber. He had a problem on his hands to tax even the Hawk's faculties. That some kind of skullduggery was going on in connection with the building of the new railroad line, he was confident; but as to just what it was, how it was functioning, or why, he was not at all certain.

"Why in blazes does a highly certificated engineer, such as Frank Allison undoubtedly is, lead Taylor to believe that he is nothing more than a run-of-mine surveyor and field man?" he demanded of the passing growth. "That doesn't make sense a-tall. What is he to gain by that? Of course there's the chance that he might have made a bad blunder on some big job and in consequence have been practically blackballed in engineering circles and because of that is hiding his identity here in the outlands until he gets a new start; but why hide his knowledge? That wouldn't be necessary. He wouldn't hafta reveal his college or previous connections. Many a good engineer has come up that hard way and never went to college. Started as a lineman or rodman, studied, gained experience, built himself up so he could hold a good job.

"Nope, it shore doesn't make sense. And why is he fooling Taylor as to those borings? What has he to gain by that? Or is he fooling himself. It doesn't look hardly possible for a man of his undoubted ability, but mebbe *he* turned the work over to a subordinate and went on a drunk or something and didn't check the results carefully. And mebbe it doesn't make much dif'rence anyhow. There is undoubtedly a clay bed beneath the muck of the swamp, and the clay should base on bedrock or other firm foundationing. And, after all, as Taylor pointed out, they're not anchoring piers or building towers. There should be plenty of support for the roadbed, once they do a good job of filling, with plenty of good piling driven and the right amount of shoring.

"Still, it all looks funny. Mebbe old Keith Gordon *is* right about that darned Quag. Well, we'd oughta soon find out. Going to have rain, too, it looks like, and if it's a big one, that should help test the thing out. Well, I can't go maverickin' to Taylor or somebody and start bawling that I gotta hunch something isn't all 'bove board. If old Jaggers Dunn, the C & P General Manager, were just on the ground, I could talk to him, and he'd get to the bottom of things if anybody could. But that's out for the present, with Dunn swallerforkin' 'round over Europe. Oh, well, I got some real work cut out for me."

His face grew even more sternly bleak as he turned his mind to the problem to which the railroad and its possible difficulties was vastly subordinate. There was nothing theoretical about the Shotgun Riders. Slade had plenty of positive proof of the existence of the villainous band. Their apprehension or extermination was his first and paramount task as a Ranger. His thoughts turned to Bunch Mawson, the salty looking foreman of the ZTI.

"Why did Mawson lie about the cowboy Crip Bayles?" he wondered. "He was plumb positive in saying that Bayles left the XTI on the four-teenth of the month."

From his pocket he drew the blood smeared bit of paper he had taken from the shirt pocket of the cowboy's pitiful corpse. With narrowed eyes he stared at the clearly written date—the Twenty-second of September. Bayles had received the statement of his advances eight days after Mawson maintained he had severed his connections with the spread. Also, Mawson had risen to the bait when Slade mentioned working with Bayles in the Cochise country: Mawson had immediately intimated that he, Mawson, also knew of Bayles' Cochise origins, a figment of the Hawk's imagina-tion. What was Mawson covering up? Did he have something to do with the murder of Bayles, the potential informer? Was Mawson the black-eyed leader of the Shotgun Riders spotted by the wounded watchman Andrews as he lay apparently dead in the ditch?

Slade asked himself these questions, but for the moment he declined to hazard answers. He pulled up as he reached the spot where the trail forked, and stared long and earnestly westward along the branch that wound away toward the bleak Paloma Mountains.

"We gotta take a little look-see over in those hills," he told Shadow as he rode northward to Cienaga Valley.

Chapter 18

Slade was busy at the ranch for several days, and when he and his cowboys drove the second herd to the construction camp, the grading had already moved out upon the Quag.

It was a thrilling and fascinating scene. Huge dredges ripped and tore at the green surface, shearing away the thick rind of peaty earth, laying bare the black ooze that seethed and bubbled below the grass roots. Beneath the many, many feet of ooze was a watery belt of sand, and under that the firm stiff clay Duncan Taylor relied upon for a foundation bed.

The scrapers, dredges and shovels excavated a wide, deep ditch into which the pile drivers hammered the massive piles. Then carload after carload of crushed stone rumbled down about and over the piles. Yard by yard the long causeway crept forward, wide at the bottom, bulwarked by piles and concrete shoring, narrowing at the top to the width necessary for ties and rails. And ties were laid and rails spiked into place at once, so that the cars loaded with stone and other materials would ever be hard on the heels of the dredgers and pile drivers.

Duncan Taylor, spattered with mud, but with his eyes jumping excitedly behind the lenses of his glasses, indicated the fine points of the work to Slade.

"And they said it couldn't be done!" he crowed. "Well, we're doing it! What do you say now, Gordon?"

But Keith Gordon gazed at the work with somber eyes, and shook his big head.

"She'll never stand, Taylor," he said with a finality that for the moment dampened even the ardor of the enthusiastic engineer.

Slade, glancing at the silent, impassive Allison, who stood nearby, surprised the shadow of a smile flitting across his bulkily handsome florid face. And it seemed to the Hawk that there was a derisive sparkle far down in the inscrutable depths of the assistant's black eyes.

"Who's he laughing at?" mused Slade, "Gordon —or Taylor?"

But as the dredges and shovels roared and clattered and the pile drivers quivered the earth with their ponderous blows, the laugh appeared to be definitely on Gordon. The yards of completed grade and spiked rails grew to rods, to furlongs; and when Slade returned to the scene of operations, after busy days of combing the brakes and canyons of the Slash K for elusive dogies, a full mile of shining steel slashed the vivid green of the gut. Duncan Taylor wore a triumphant grin that seemed to stretch his mouth from ear to ear, but again Slade surprised that elusive, expectant glitter in the depths of Frank Allison's dark eyes.

Temporary spurs and sidings had been laid upon the Quag, for the dredges showed a thickness of rind over the muck that encouraged Taylor to take a chance and thereby speed the work.

"I wouldn't risk the subsidence or shifting with anything permanent," the engineer confided to Slade, "but by keeping a close check on the condition of the surface, we can use these spurs for running out material and machinery. Look, we've got whole strings of cars ready to dump, and a number of dredges and drivers working on the mainline right-of-way from these sidings. Mr. Dunn will be able to run the *Winona*, his big private car, into Cienaga Valley when he arrives."

"Hope so," Slade agreed.

But somehow he was not as optimistic as Taylor. Just why he could not have said there was really nothing upon which he could put his finger—but Walt Slade, like many men who ride alone down the years with only constant danger as a stirrup companion, had developed to an uncanny degree that sixth sense which might be called "presentiment," which warns of evil present or approaching when, to all outward appearances, everything is peace and security. Right now that unseen, unheard monitor deep in his brain was setting up a clamor, warning him not to be deceived or lulled into a false security, that all was not well.

But ever the scrapers and dredges ripped and tore the unresistant earth, the pile drivers thundered and the air was filled with the ringing clash of steel on steel. And ever the Black Quag, vividly, lushly green after the heavy rains of a week before, stretched silent and inscrutable from wall to wall of the narrow valley mouth. Once only did the Quag manifest its ominous power.

Walt Slade was on the scene at the time, and only his quick wit and instant action prevented tragedy as black as the ooze of the Quag.

A workman had moved out upon the Quag some little distance from the right-of-way. He was turning to retrace his steps toward the fill, when suddenly he sank into the earth to his waist. His startled yell turned all eyes in his direction. Several of his fellow workers started toward him, but the Hawk's thunderous shout halted them in their tracks.

"Back!" he roared. "Keep away from him. He's stepped on a thin spot, and if you go to him you'll be sucked in, too."

The unfortunate victim was howling his terror as he sank deeper and deeper in the shifting muck. Madly he twisted and scrambled, clawing to the ground, pulling out fistfuls of grass as he strove frantically to draw his body from the clinging oozes. The earth crumbled off at the edges, widening the hole into which he sank;

the loosely rooted grass refused him purchase. His yells took on a hysterical note of despair. He clutched at emptiness with upraised hands.

Something swished through the air in a snaky coil. A tight loop settled over the upraised arms and bit into the flesh under the armpits as Walt Slade instantly took his dallies about the horn and the trained Shadow tautened the twine.

But it was touch and go, even after the Ranger's expert cast had successfully lassoed the struggling man. The Quag was reluctant to give up its victim. The sucking mud clung to his body with a vacuum grip. He yelled in agony as the grass rope seared his flesh. The yell choked off in a gulping gurgle as Shadow moved back a steady step at a time and the noose tightened more and more about his chest.

"It's cuttin' me in two!" he managed to squawk with a last breath.

"Part of you is coming out then, anyway," the Ranger told him grimly. "Hang onto the rope with yore hands, and save yore breath—you'll need it."

Seconds later the unconscious man was drawn out upon the grass, the muck sucking and gurgling angrily as it swirled into the space his body vacated. Slade cautiously sent Shadow back a few more steps before he motioned the workmen to run forward and loosen the noose.

"You're foolin' with dynamite here, feller,"

Slade told Duncan Taylor as the engineer panted up to the scene of the rescue. "Keep yore men off that damn swamp. There's no way to tell where the thin places are, and if a man goes down he's done for if he doesn't get help pronto."

Taylor stared at the dark hole where the ooze still rippled with sluggish coilings and slow eddies; his peering eyes were sober and respectful.

"You're right," he agreed. "The damn thing's deadly; but we'll whip it yet."

But Walt Slade, as he rode slowly toward the trail which led to town, was suddenly not so sure. There was something ominously terrible about this still expanse of poisonous green. The Quag seemed to crouch like a waiting monster, sullen, venomous, patient, biding its time, gathering its strength to strike.

Chapter 19

When Slade arrived at Keith Gordon's *cantina*, Clate Shaw, the recently appointed sheriff, was just leaving the office. The Ranger had a drink at the bar with Ward, the head bartender, conversed with the drink juggler for a few minutes and then knocked at the office door. Gordon called to him to enter and he sat down on the opposite side of the table and rolled a cigarette. For some time he and Gordon discussed range matters, then Slade regaled his employer with an account of the near tragedy at the railhead. Gordon shook his head pessimistically.

"The Quag is just feeling them out," he declared. "When it's all good and ready, it'll cut loose proper. Slade, I'm beginning to think of that damn swamp as something alive—viciously alive—something that can wait and watch until the proper moment arrives. Have you felt it?"

Slade nodded. "Hafta admit I have," he replied. "I'm afraid we're letting things get us jumpy, Gordon. We'll be seeing things and pickin' 'em outa the air next."

"That's what Clate Shaw said just now," Gordon remarked, "only he wasn't talking about the Quag. He dropped in to tell me he's sent a couple of deputies up to the mines to escort the bi-monthly gold shipment to town. It's a big one, biggest for a long time, and mighty valuable. The shipping time has been kept a dead secret. Only myself and Shaw know it's leaving the mines today. They don't know it up there, even, except the manager and one or two trusted clerks and guards. Can't afford to take any chances with that damn Shotgun Rider outfit on the loose hereabouts."

Walt Slade suddenly sat up straight in his chair. "When does the shipment leave the mines?" he asked quietly.

"Should be leaving about now, I imagine," Gordon replied. "The deputies would have arrived at the mine early this afternoon, and that was all they were waiting for up there. Why?"

Slade stood up, his face bleak. "Get yore horse," he said tersely. "Get heeled, too— holster guns and a rifle in the boot. We're riding."

"What! What!" Gordon exclaimed, his eyes widening. "You mean to say you think—"

"I mean to say we've got to sift sand if that gold shipment is to get to the bank," Slade interrupted grimly. "Trail yore rope, feller, we can talk as we ride. We're mighty liable to be too late as it is."

Together they hurried from the saloon, Gordon still expostulating.

"But I tell you nobody but Shaw and trusted officials at the mine know the shipment is leaving today," he sputtered. "The stage makes a regular run from the mines every other day and nobody will think anything of it pulling out. The deputies left town before daylight and took a roundabout route to allay suspicion and fool any possible watchers. That shipment is perfectly safe."

"We'll decide that when the gold is in the bank vault," Slade replied. "Here's the hitch rack. I'll wait here until you grab yore cayuse."

Two hours later they were climbing the winding trail that led to the Tonto Pass, through which ran the route to the mines farther to the northwest in the hills.

Slade glanced at the towering rock walls of the pass and estimated the grade with a trained eye.

"Isn't hard to see why Taylor hates to use this route for his railroad," the Ranger observed. "It would be a tough job of grading."

"But when he got his road built, he'd have a line that would stay where he put it," Gordon replied obstinately.

"You say the original survey was by way of the Pass?" Slade asked.

"Gordon nodded. "Yes, but when Taylor sent Frank Allison ahead with the advance force, Allison ran a line through Cienaga Valley. When Taylor arrived, Allison had figures to show him. Then he took Taylor on a tour over the Cienaga Valley route and sold him the idea of running the line through the valley and on by way of

Feather Canyon to the mines. I went to Taylor, and so did other oldtimers, and warned him against the Quag; but Taylor had Allison take borings, and he insisted that the borings showed a clay bed under the muck of sufficient firmness to support the road."

"And they didn't bore beyond the clay?" Slade asked a question to which he already had the answer, with the purpose of drawing Gordon out.

"That's the whole trouble," the other replied vigorously. "I tell you, Slade, there's something under that clay besides bedrock as Taylor and Allison maintain. More muck and quicksand, the chances are."

"Muck and quicksand would not support a heavy layer of clay, even if they formed beneath the clay, which is highly improbable," Slade pointed out.

"That buoyed weight vanished at a point far below the extent Allison grants the clay layer," Gordon countered. "Oh, I know they say that was an isolated sinkhole or fissure," he added quickly, "but just the same nothing that has ever sunk in the Quag has been recovered, or even touched. Remember, old Don Martin's big *casa* and barns sank out of sight and nobody has ever seen a sign of them since."

"Granting that the story of Don Martin is anything but a tall yarn that grew a heap taller as it passed down through the years," Slade observed.

Gordon shrugged his heavy shoulders. "Oh, well, let's forget it," he grunted wearily. "Here we are in the pass, half way to the mines, and not a sign of anything wrong."

"And no sign of the stage, either," Slade pointed out. "Don't you think they had oughta gotten this far by now?"

"Maybe, if they started on time," Gordon admitted. "Perhaps they were delayed at the last minute by something."

For nearly two miles they rode swiftly through the level pass, the tall cliffs frowning on either side and shutting out most of the light, so that the great gorge was gloomy, with pools of deep shadow at the base of its walls. West of the pass the trail dipped sharply, winding between bristles of spruce and mountain beeches. The incline leveled off somewhat a mile farther on and Gordon said that soon the bottom of the wide hollow would be reached and the trail would climb once more.

The growth edged closer to the trail as it neared bottom and increased in density, a tangled wall that shut off vision and much of sound.

"At the bottom of the hollow there's a fork," Gordon remarked. "The left fork dips southward and into a wild canyon on its way to Mexico. It used to be a smuggling route, and probably still is."

Another half mile, with the horses picking their

way among gullies and boulders scoured out by the rains. Slade suddenly raised his head in an attitude of listening. Gordon heard it, too, a popping and crackling like two dry sticks burning in a dry fire.

"What the blazes?" he muttered.

Slade tightened his bridle hand, and his face grew bleak.

"That's rifle fire ahead," he rapped brittlely. "Let's go, feller. Trail, Shadow, trail."

He slid his heavy Winchester from the saddle boot as he spoke. Gordon followed suit.

Weaving, zigzagging, to avoid the gullies and washes, their irons clashing on the white flint stones and rattling the loose boulders, the horses thundered down the grade. Ahead the trail dipped and writhed, with seldom a clear view of a hundred yards affording. The steady crackle of the distant rifles intensified. Soon faint shouts came to the riders' ears.

Gordon was swearing with excitement, his voice ringing like a bell. Slade was grimly silent, his eyes, coldly gray, staring intently ahead. Shadow snorted, laid his ears back and fairly poured his long body over the broken ground, taxing Gordon's big roan to keep abreast of him. In fact, it was but Slade's lightly restraining hand on the bridle that prevented the great black from leaving the other far behind.

The trail veered sharply through dense growth,

then straightened out with whipsnap abruptness. Shadow's irons clashed and rang as Slade put his backward leaning weight on the bridle. Gordon likewise pulled up.

A hundred yards ahead the trail dipped sharply into the very trough of the hollow. On the far side it writhed steeply upward, losing itself almost instantly in a tangle of tall chaparal. A heavy vehicle coming down the far slope would be coming fast with screeching brakes and horses moving swiftly to clear the shove of tongue and single trees.

That, without a doubt, was the way the lumbering stagecoach from the mines had swept around the sharp bend and smack into two heavy tree trunks that had been felled across the trail. A horse was down in a wild welter of tangled harness. His fellows were plunging frantically, snorting with fear, but unable to free themselves. The stage itself was slewed around with a rear wheel mired in a deep gulley. From behind the stalled coach spurted puffs of smoke. And snug in the shelter of the fallen trees, a line of figures crouched with blazing rifles, methodically raking the coach with a withering fire.

Through the thin panels tore the heavy slugs, and it was only a matter of time until the besieged defenders of the gold shipment would be struck down, even though they were hidden from the sight of the attackers.

At the sound of drumming hoofs behind them, several of the bandits wheeled with shouts of alarm and warning. The foremost pitched onto his face as a slug from Slade's rifle tore through his throat. A second howled with pain and pawed at a blood spouting shoulder. The others fired wildly at the mounted pair.

With whoops of joy at this evidence of approaching help, two men leaped from behind the stage and ran forward, aiming and firing as fast as they could.

That was enough for the drygulchers. Caught between two fires, they broke and scattered, fleeing madly toward a clump of plunging horses that were held in check by two of the band\ where the south fork of the trail dipped into the brush.

Grimly, the Hawk lined sights with one of the men holding the horses.

"Get those hellions and the horses will bolt," Slade muttered as his eyes glanced along the rifle barrel and his finger tightened on the trigger.

But even as the hammer fell, Shadow squealed with rage and pain and plunged so wildly as to nearly upseat his rider. Slade held to the hull by a mighty effort and shouted to soothe the horse. Blood was welling from a jagged furrow in the fleshly part of the black's soft foreleg and he was dancing with the pain.

Slade emptied the magazine of his rifle at the

fleeing robbers, but it was like shooting from the deck of a pitching ship. Gordon, who was evidently anything but a marksman, managed to shoot a man through the arm and knock a gun from the hand of another. Then his rifle jammed and he raved curses as he tried to free the wedged cartridge.

The men who had run from behind the stage were not able to get in line for a shot before the outlaws flung themselves onto the backs of their horses and rode madly down the south fork of the trail, vanishing instantly amid the growth, leaving one of their number sprawled in the dust before the felled trees.

Grating a bitter oath, Slade shoved his smoking rifle into the boot and swung down from the hull. With his horse bleeding and limping, pursuit was out of the question. He examined Shadow's wound and was devoutly thankful to find it was nothing that rest and care would not cure.

"It'll be healed up in a coupla weeks, old-timer," he soothed the snorting horse.

Shadow whickered softly and thrust his muzzle into the palm of Slade's hand, as if explaining he could not help what had happened. Slade tweaked his ears affectionately and then proceeded to bind up the wound with his own handkerchief. Before he had finished, the stage driver and one of Clate Shaw's deputies gabbled up.

"Feller, you saved the gold!" exclaimed the

driver. "Pity you couldn't get here in time to save pore Chuck Wilson—he's inside the coach, drilled dead center by the fust lead those sidewinders throwed."

The remaining deputy ground his teeth at mention of the fate of his companion.

"The jolt when the rear wheel dropped into that gulley as Russ locked the front ones throwed him and me clean off the box, or we'd got it same as Chuck," he explained. "My back's bad sprained and Russ has got a wrenched knee, but otherwise I reckon we're fulla beans and kickin'. How'd you fellers happen to be along this way?"

Slade did not answer the question immediately. After assuring himself that the deputy inside the coach was beyond human aid, he carefully examined the body of the dead robber.

"Any of you fellers know him?" he asked of the group peering over his shoulder.

There was a general shaking of heads. "You winged a coupla more of them," the deputy exulted.

Slade nodded absently. He was staring at the dead man's laced boots. They were not the kind of boots generally worn by horsemen, and the lower lace holes were plugged with dried and very black mud. His gaze shifted to the sunburned face and the shock of unkempt sandy hair.

"Load him inter the coach and we'll take him to town," Slade directed. "There's nothing in his pockets to show who he is or where he came from."

He stood up, and suddenly strode toward the south fork of the trail. Where the outlaw's horses had plunged and reared, he stopped and retrieved something that lay almost hidden in the edge of the growth. It was a double-barrelled, sawed-off shotgun.

The others stared at the vicious looking weapon as Slade held it up to view. The deputy wet his suddenly dry lips with his tongue. The old driver brushed a shaking hand across his eyes. Keith Gordon's huge mouth set in an expression of merciless ferocity.

"You were right again, as usual, Slade," he said uietly. "It was them—the Shotgun Riders!"

Chapter 20

Clate Shaw swore luridly when the stage pulled in bearing the slain deputy and the body of the drygulcher.

"I'm gonna ride up to the mine fust thing in the mawnin'," he stormed. "Somebody's gonna suffer for this day's work. I'll find out where the leak is up there if I hafta take the hull outfit apart. Why didn't you come to me in the fust place, Gordon?"

Keith Gordon's pale eyes glittered and his big mouth straightened out in a hard line, but at a warning glance from Slade he held his peace.

"I'll leave Shadow at Bart Coster's stable for a spell," the Ranger told Gordon. "Bart's a pretty good veterinarian, I understand, and he'll put the black hellion in shape pronto."

"You can ride my horse to the spread," Gordon told his foreman. "Send one of the boys back with him."

Slade rode to the Slash K the following morning. Sitting Gordon's big horse atop the sloping wall of the gut, where the trail ran, he paused to stare down at the scene of activity on the valley floor. Less than a mile of track was still to be laid before the crossing of the Quag was complete. The dredges chattered, the pile drivers boomed and the smoke of puffing locomotives rose through the clear air. Men swarmed like ants over the fill that slowly crept forward. There was a cheery tooting of whistles, shouts, relayed orders, the rasp of shovels and the clang of spike mauls.

And ever the yellowish green of the Quag stretched on either side, like a jaundiced eye brooding between swollen lids, malevolent, and patiently waiting.

For a long moment *El Halcon* stared down into the green depths, and when he rode on north, his face was somber, brooding. The sense of impending evil was stronger than ever, and the warning voice within his mind refused to be stilled.

And with savage force, with numbing unexpectedness and awful terror, the Quag struck. No warning presaged the blow. There was no sign of unrest beneath the still blanket of green. The autumn sun smiled down, the air was crisp and invigorating. All nature seemed at peace, with a calm peace that mocked the feverish strivings, the hurried effort and the insignificant accomplishment of the human ants swarming in the narrow gut between the steeply sloping walls of dark stone.

Walt Slade and Keith Gordon were riding to town. They intended to stop at the construction camp for a conference with Duncan Taylor. Atop the slope they paused, even as Slade had paused some days before, to stare down at the activity below. One long leg hooked comfortably over the horn, the Hawk rolled a cigarette with the slim fingers of his left hand, lighted it deftly and drew in a deep and satisfying lungful of fragrant smoke. He glanced at Gordon, who was gazing with reluctant admiration at the progress made by the road builders. Gordon turned to speak, but at that instant the Ranger stiffened erect and held up a hand for silence.

Far to the north, between the lofty valley walls, had birthed a strange and weird sound that slithered through the drone of the road building like a hot lance through shrinking flesh.

It began as a sibilant hissing miles away, sped swiftly up the valley, gaining in volume of sound until it was like to the wide open vent of a steam boiler under high pressure, rising to a grinding roar. With a noise like a great locomotive it thundered by the tense listeners on the top of the slope and passed into the south, ending in a terrific booming and blasting deep within the tortured earth. The cliff top rocked and shuddered.

A silence fell, broken by the startled yells of the workers below. Again the sound, quivering the air, dinning against the eardrums until they rang with a timbre as of hammered steel. Again the awful silence, through which knifed Keith Gordon's shout. His voice broke in a high-pitched scream of nerves strained to the snapping point.

"The Quag! Look at the Quag!"

Slade stared down into the gut, his own face blanching. With a rattling crash a pile driver went over. A huge steam shovel followed as the earth beneath it dipped and swayed. A locomotive slid crazily from the track and clanged over on its side, steam bellowing from broken pipes and loosened joints. Men, howling their terror, were running madly from the right-of-way, where the new fill was cracking and buckling.

Wide fissures rent the packed and pounded causeway of crushed stone and steel piles. Rails twisted and coiled as giant ribbons. Up-ended crossties jutted forth like splintered teeth from a torn mouth. Men caught in the wreckage shrieked with agony and fright.

The whole green surface of the Quag was moving with a slow undulation, but the focus of disturbance was the long white scar of the fill.

"I told you so!" screamed Keith Gordon. "Look! Look!"

The fill was sinking, slowly, inexorably. A swirl of sluggish ooze suddenly lapped over a segment of the white ribbon. Other gashes of glistening black appeared. The long line of the fill seemed to writhe and arch like the severed parts of a chopped-up snake. Less and less of the white line of stone and piling remained, and the swirling black of the ooze swiftly lengthened.

211

"Come on!" Slade shouted savagely, "we may be able to do something."

At a dead run they sent their horses along the trail, for the slopes were too steep to ride down. The animals snorted and quivered with abject fear. Their instincts sensed that unknown terrors were abroad, forces beyond their comprehension; atavistic terrors of the far dim days of earth's youngness when seething tar pools engulfed giant monsters of prehistoric times and embalmed their mighty forms so that their terrific skeletons would startle the eyes of men after the streams that rippled past their tombs had been frozen by ten thousand times ten thousand winters and thawed by as many returning springs.

Smoking, panting, drenched with sweat, the horses floundered to halt at the mouth of the valley, where the green blanket of the Quag began. Slade swung to the ground and unhesitatingly stepped onto the surface of the Quag.

"My God, man, you're taking your life into your hands!" Keith Gordon protested, but nevertheless he followed the Ranger out upon the treacherous surface.

But before they had covered half the length of the swirling black trough that had been the line of the fill, Slade realized that there was nothing to be done. A score of workmen had been swallowed by the clutching ooze. Black holes, full of liquid mud, yawned where shovel and pile driver and locomotive had sunk from sight. Some of the spur tracks and sidings still stood, but there were marked signs of subsidence there also, amply attested to by buckling rails and sagging ties.

Even as Slade and Gordon skirted the spot, a stretch of track upon which stood a locomotive and a string of cars loaded with crushed stone sank silently from view. The mud bubbled and boiled about the hot boiler and firebox for a moment; then the glistening surface smoothed out save for swirls and ripples to the accompaniment of reptilian suckings and gurglings.

"Nothing can stand on the Quag," Keith Gordon kept muttering, adding in a shaking voice, "And the Quag never gives up its dead!"

Men stumbled past the approaching pair, men who gabbed and mouthed incoherently, frozen horror distorting their white faces, the black muck of the Quag clinging to their clothes and hands. Slade reached out and gripped Duncan Taylor as he reeled drunkenly past, his eyes filmed and unseeing. The Ranger shook him vigorously.

"Nobody else left alive," the engineer mumbled in answer to Slade's question. "I stayed until the last man was on the move. I don't know how many we lost—hafta check the rolls to find out. We didn't dredge deep enough. The fill slid sideways. Water washed the earth away from the piles, I guess. We'll beat the damn thing yet!"

Keith Gordon drew a deep breath. "You'll never beat the Quag," he said with quiet emphasis. "Aren't you convinced yet, Taylor? Are you going to risk more equipment and more lives? You might as well try to sweep back the sea."

Duncan Taylor's stubborn jaw jutted forward. "We'll beat it yet!" he repeated, dully, and stumbled on after the last of his men.

Gordon stared grimly at the engineer's retreating back.

"He doesn't know it yet, but he's done," he remarked with quiet finality.

"How's that?" Slade asked.

Gordon gestured toward the sucking mud. "Look at the equipment that is lost," he said, "thousands and thousands of dollars worth— cost tens of thousands to replace it—to say nothing of the cost of the material that went to the making of the fill—more thousands. When he wires in his report to the main office, he'll mighty soon learn that the money set aside for the building of this line is down to bedrock. There's not anywhere near enough to replace this loss.

"The C & P undertook to build this line under very exacting conditions. The road will not replace the money lost without taking over the stock we hold in the line. In other words, we fellows who went into this deal will lose all we put into it, as I told you before. Frankly, I am of the opinion the line will be abandoned unless we can finance further construction, and a swell chance we've got of doing that!

"We may, some of us, be able to save our spreads. Thanks largely to you because of the way you got more marketable cattle together than I had any notion I had, and by saving that gold shipment from the mine, I believe I can meet my payments when they come due. Otherwise I would lose my outfit and business to the bank. But the money I put into the road, and it was plenty! I'll lose every cent of that."

Slade turned and glanced up the valley. "The road had oughta go through," he said. "It's needed over here, needed bad. Yes, it had oughta go through. Perhaps we'll get a break of some sort and be able to save it yet." He stared at the long ditch filled with sluggish black ooze. "Something queer about this darn section of skimmed-over hell," he muttered. "Something almighty queer about everything connected with it. I'm beginning to have a vague sorta notion about it, Gordon, but I'm darned if I have any idea how to play this booming hunch."

"But right now I got a little chore of my own to 'tend to," he added as if to himself.

His face was bleak, his eyes cold as he turned his gaze toward the grim hills in the north.

Chapter 21

Work on the railroad was at a standstill. Many of the workmen drifted away from the scene, some finding employment in the mines, some loafing in town until their money should be exhausted, others starting out on prospecting trips or leaving the section altogether.

Duncan Taylor held long conferences, by wire, with the C & P main office. He held other conferences in Cienaga with the local backers of the road and Wade Thorne, president and controller of the Cienaga Bank. They were futile conferences, Keith Gordon told Slade. Thorne could not see his way clear to advance more money with the Cienaga Valley ranches as security, and said so frankly.

"He's acting mighty decent about it, though," Gordon assured the Ranger. "He says he has no intention of pushing anybody for immediate payment or of foreclosing so long as there is a reasonable expectation of their being able to pay. I wonder, Slade, if that Dallas bank could have made a mistake when they wired you that they had never heard of Wade Thorne and had never had any dealings with him?"

"Might be," Slade admitted, "but they were

mighty positive in their answer to my wire. You read the answer."

"Thorne has always appeared open and above board since he settled in the community," Gordon insisted.

"He might have had a past to cover up," Slade hazarded. "Many a gent who has turned over a new leaf has hadda lay low about his early life. If you 'vestigated all the big ranch owners of the Southwest as to how they started their herds, the chances are you'd uncover some funny things. Many a big outfit had its beginning in steers slipped across the line from Mexico, steers the *Dons* down the other side of the river never got paid for; and more'n one paying mine was a claim jumped by salty young hombres who later became substantial citizens. Nope, you mustn't allus condemn a feller for what he did in his young days when his blood was over hot and his notions were still sorta fuzzy."

With the thinning out of the construction camp, much less meat was needed and the boys at the Slash K were not overly busy for the moment. Walt Slade, however, was very busy. Day after day he rode the hills to the west and north, seeking some clue that might lead him to the hangout of the dread Shotgun Riders, for he was confident that the sinister band had head-quarters somewhere in this wild hole-in-the-wall country. A number of days had passed in fruitless and wearisome riding, however, before he encountered the first positive evidence that his hunch might have a solid foundation.

Again hovering vultures led him to the body of a man. But this time it was the remains of a man who had been buried in a too-shallow grave. Coyotes had dug up the body, and what the furtive little "wolves" had passed over, the vultures had about finished. What interested the Hawk, however, was the indubitable fact that the man had been buried at a comparatively recent date and that his right shoulder had been smashed and broken by a heavy bullet. Before Slade's eyes rose a vision of one of the dry-gulchers of the gold bearing stagecoach pawing frantically at a blood spouting shoulder.

"The hellion cashed in while they were high-tailing," he muttered staring at the shattered bones. "The outfit didn't dare leave his body where it might be found in case we tried to run them down, so they buried him. They figgered they'd need to be in one hell of a hurry and skimped the job. Didn't bed him down with boulders and didn't dig deep enough. Coyotes smelled him out."

With the greatest care he quartered the ground near the grave, and paused where a horse's iron had scored deeply in a soft spot.

"Uh-huh, I figgered they wouldn't move far from their trail to dig," he exulted. "Let's see, now, this shoe mark shows they were headed nawth, and moving fast. Let's go!"

He forked the sturdy bay he was riding, (Shadow was still taking it easy in the Slash K horse corral, although he was about fit for service once more) and moved slowly along in line with the hoof mark. A little later he discovered other imprints, and further on still more.

The trail of the fleeing drygulchers was faint, with only an occasional hoof scar where a soft spot of ground replaced the ordinarily rocky soil, or a broken twig dangled to point to the recent passage of a body of horsemen; but it was ample for so expert a tracker as the Hawk. Mile upon mile, Walt Slade followed the scent with uncanny skill, his keen eyes missing no sign, however slight. And deeper and deeper the trail bored into the grim gorges of the northern hills. Finally it led into a gloomy canyon with towering walls and a floor matted with growth.

And here the Ranger gained assurance. Here a horseman was obliged to force his way through tangled bush, and the distinctly marked trac that wound into the canyon's depths could never have been made by a hunting animal. Down the center of the gorge flowed a sizeable stream of water, and beside the stream was the indubitable evidence that horses had passed this way time and again.

Hot on the scent, his pulses pounding with

excitement of the chase, Slade rode into the depths of the canyon, his ears straining for any chance sound, his keen glance darting from brush clump to boulder. But it was his nose that first told him that he was not alone in the gorge. Borne on a chance breeze came a pungent whiff of wood smoke. Instantly the Ranger pulled up, peering, listening. The narrow track wound on before him, void of sound or movement, the grim walls frowned on either side of the almost equally dense wall of thorny growth.

And then suddenly there was sound—the sound of horses swiftly approaching, from behind!

For a crawling instant, Slade sat tense and undecided. To force his way through the brush which walled the trail, without making a prodigious racket, was impossible, and he doubted that the bay would face the thorns. Even if he did, the chance of escape that way was negligible. Progress would of necessity be slow, and the outlaws, doubtless familiar with the ground, would be able to hunt the fugitive down at their leisure. To turn and ride back the way he had come was madness.

No, in a bold gamble lay his only hope. He put spurs to the bay and sent him flying along the narrow track. Grimly he peered ahead, gun hand ready for a lightning draw. Another whiff of smoke, stronger this time, then a fragrant smell of steaming coffee and frying meat. Another moment and he had burst into a small clearing on the banks of the stream. A clearing in which stood three roughly built cabins. From the chimney of one, smoke was coiling. In the doorway lounged a man, and other men stood nearby. Several horses saddled, with reins looped up, were cropping the long grass.

All this Slade noted in a single swift glance. Like a distorted vision from a dream, the big bay flashed across the clearing. There was a startled yell, then a wild shouting. Slade drew, and sent a storm of bullets whining about the astounded men. They ducked madly, running this way and that, and before they could recover their scrambled sense, horse and rider were nearly to the shelter of growth on the far side of the clearing.

But before they reached it, guns were cracking behind them. Slade heard the vicious whine of passing lead, felt the wind of a slug that came alarmingly close. Then his heart leaped to a sodden thud and a scream of pain from his horse. The bay floundered in his stride, stumbled, leaped forward with a last spasmodic effort. For nearly a quarter of a mile he flew along the bushy trail, gasping, sobbing, blowing a bloody foam from his flaring nostrils. Then with a deep groan he faltered, slowed, sank to his knees and rolled over, dead!

Slade freed his feet from the stirrups and sprang

clear of the faithful animal's death struggles. For a fleeting instant he stood straining his ears. Almost immediately his keen hearing caught the click of fast hoofs on the trail behind.

Grimly he set out along the trail at a dead run. He heard the pursuit pause for a moment beside the body of the horse, then come on again with a clashing of hoofs and a babble of shouts. On either side the dense growth hemmed him in, a thorny wall, almost impenetrable. To attempt to force his way through was futile, and nothing would be gained by holding up in the brush. His only hope of escape lay in keeping to the trail and ahead of the pursuit until some spot where he could make an effectual stand hove into view. Head well up, elbows against his sides, he ran easily with long, lithe strides.

The high heels of his boots hampered him and the weight of his heavy chaps did not help; but with unfaltering strength he sped along at a pace that, for the moment at least, kept him ahead of the horsemen and out of their sight around the brush-flanked bends. He knew that the pursuers would not come on recklessly, fearing possible ambush that would take toll before the death was sounded over the quarry.

On and on! Slade was breathing heavily now and the calves of his legs were beginning to burn and ache with fatigue. The click of irons sounded nearer, and the vengeful shouts of the pursuers. He rounded a final bend, the growth fell away on either hand and he was running up a narrowing gorge hemmed in on either side by towering rocky walls. Ahead the stream emptied into a swirling pool that apparently had no outlet. The pool washed the rock wall to the right, and also the end wall of the gorge, which was a beetling cliff directly over the pool and a broken and shattering slope to the left.

As he ran, Slade studied the slope. To attempt to pick his way up the tortuous face was out of the question. Long before he reached the top, he would be shot down. The side walls of the gorge were sheer, the cliff face at the end of the gorge equally sheer.

For a despairing moment, Slade faltered in his stride. With grim finality his hands dropped to the black butts of his guns. He would turn like a wolf at bay and take what toll he could before the Shotgun Riders scored their victory. His eyes were icily gray, his face bleak and drawn. Then suddenly the eyes, which had been mechanically searching the cliff face ahead, blazed with reborn hope. Winding up the face of the cliff was a shallow fissure. The fissure, so far as he could see from below, ended at a jutting ledge no great distance from the beetling summit of the cliff, and to the Ranger's trained glance it appeared that the ledge sloped inward.

If this were true, there was a chance that he

might hole up behind the natural parapet until darkness provided an added opportunity to escape. Anyhow, it was worth trying. With a last frantic burst of speed he darted forward and an instant later was climbing the fissure that wound upward at a shallow angle. He was half way to the crest before the pursuit burst through the growth and into view.

For a moment there was a frustrated babble from the Riders. The fugitive had apparently vanished. Then a triumphant yell denoted the discovery of the climbing figure dimly outlined in the shadowy fissure.

Guns began to blaze; but the range was great and the target an elusive blur against the dark stone. Bullets spatted the cliff, showering Slade with bits of lead and stinging rock fragments. One grazed his cheek, another ripped through the sleeves of his shirt. The jarring smack of a third as it glanced from his boot heel almost hurled him to the rocks seventy feet below. In another instant, however, he had swarmed over the lip of the ledge and wriggled to comparative safety.

As he had anticipated, the ledge was deeply indented, sloping back to the cliff face for a distance of about ten feet. From there on to the crest, another seventy feet or so higher up, the cliff face was sheer. Far, far below, for the fissure had trended toward the side wall of the gorge, was the dark surface of the pool, appearing from this height to be little larger than a puddle. The dark water seethed back under an overhang that almost touched the swirling ripples.

All this Slade saw in a single swift, all-embracing glance. Then he snugged low against the ledge and peered cautiously over the lip.

His pursuers had halted some distance out from the cliff, and appeared to be holding a council of war. Slade counted an even dozen as they huddled in the shadow of the brush. Lining his long barrel over the lip, he sent a shower of lead screeching toward the group. A yell of pain answered the shots and the Riders dived wildly out of sight. Almost instantly, however, bullets knocked chips from the crumbly lip of the ledge or spatted viciously against the cliff face above. Slade wriggled back out of range and proceeded to take council with himself.

So long as he remained away from the lip of the ledge, he was out of range of the marksmen in the growth. The brush grew thickly along the left wall of the gorge, but Slade did not think that even from there could the Riders reach their mark. A bulge of the cliff face sheltered him from danger in that direction. He tried to look over the lip once or twice, but each time bullets fanned his face. The men in the brush were watchful and at the same time kept themselves well hidden. It appeared to be a stalemate, with approaching darkness favoring the quarry.

But Slade was not at ease. That subtle sixth sense that so often warned of unexpected danger was stirring. Perhaps it was this undefinable but persistent monitor, or perhaps it was a flicker of shadow that caused him to suddenly glance upward. With a movement that was perfection of eye and muscle coordination, he writhed aside. As he did so, a bullet spatted into the stone floor of his shelter, showering him with stinging fragments. Over the cliff crest, seventy feet above, peered a savage face.

The roar of Slade's answering Colt was an echo to the report of the shot from above. There was a cry of agony and a body pitched over the lofty crest to land with a dreadful crash scant inches from the prostrate Ranger. From below sounded a yell of execration and a roar of shots. An instant later a huge rock thundered down from the crest.

Slade scuttled along the ledge like a crab, writhed in against the cliff face and a second boulder whizzed past and shattered to fragments at his feet. Members of the outlaw band had crept through the brush which flanked the gorge wall, clambered up the rocky slope and now held the cliff crest. The ledge which had provided a shelter was now untenable.

Bullets spattered the sloping floor as a man above pointed his gun over the edge and fired blindly. Another boulder boomed through the air and Slade barely managed to get from 'under. His mind worked at lightning speed. He could not stay on the ledge. He could not go up. He must go down! But to go down by way of the crevice was manifestly impossible. There was one other way, a frightful route, with a bare possibility of advantage at its end, if he managed to reach the end alive. He might be able to crouch in the water beneath the overhang at the base of the cliff, and, sheltered there by the arching stone, fight it out with the drygulchers.

As another boulder came hurtling over the crest, Slade surged to his feet. A wild chorus of yells from below greeted his appearance. The outlaws had swarmed out of the growth and were running forward. In their lead was a tall, black-eyed man with a handsome, livid face. Slade's eyes narrowed with instant recognition.

"So damn shore I'm done for he didn't even take the trouble to mask," the Ranger muttered as he leaped to the lip of the ledge.

For a crawling instant he poised on the crumbling edge, bullets storming around him; then, one hand pressed tightly over his mouth and nose, he leaped outward and shot down toward the pool, nearly a hundred feet below.

A hurricane of displaced air tore at his clothes. He heard the amazed whoops of the outlaws, saw the dark surface of the pool rushing up to meet him at a frightful speed. Then he struck the agitated surface with a sullen plunging splash. Foam and water geysered high into the air, curling wave crests lapped the rock wall as the ever widening rings swirled outward. Then the surface of the pool gradually regained its former tranquility disturbed only by the ceaseless seethe and ripple near the overhang of the cliff.

The Shotgun Riders rushed forward, guns ready, peering, muttering. But no sleek, black head broke surface, no stunned body "dimmered" up through the dark depths. The outlaws strained their eyes, walked along the edge of the deep pool, the bottom of which they could not see.

"Why the hell don't he come up?" one demanded querulously.

The tall leader leaned over the murky flood, stared intently, as if he sought by very will power to fathom the turbid depths. Finally he straightened and answered his follower's question.

"Wedged in between the rocks or stuck in the mud. It doesn't matter which. Come on, he's done for."

Then men who had climbed the crest joined their companions below. The band mounted and rode away, leaving the ominous pool to guard its grim secret. At the base of the cliff the shadows deepened; the dark surface remained undisturbed.

Chapter 22

When Walt Slade struck the surface of the pool, the shock was so terrific that for the moment he was dazed. His nose bled from the force with which his hand was driven against his face and it felt as if every tooth in his head were loosened. He had time for just one gasping breath before he plunged into the cruel blue depths.

Down, down he went, for the pool was deep, down until his feet struck bottom. He struggled to rise, his lungs clamoring for fresh air. But even as he surged forward, he was gripped as by a mighty hand. With relentless force he was hurled toward the iron face of the cliff, at a speed that threatened to dash the life from his body when he struck the rock.

But he didn't strike. Through the whirling murk he dimly made out a curving opening, the top of which was under water. Into this opening he was whirled, writhing, twisting, frantically seeking to break water. He did so with a plunge like a rising fish, his body hurtling nearly out of the water.

In the vague half light he had a fleeting glimpse of a dense mass of rock hanging directly over his head. Then he was whisked into black darkness. His ears were filled with the roar of rushing water, his brain whirled with the raging turmoil, waves slapped against his face, he gasped mixed air and water, coughing and strangling, borne down by the weight of his guns and his leather chaps. In fact, only the appalling force of the current kept him on the surface.

Frantically he tried to swim sideways. He might as well have tried to swim in a mill race. The current spun him around with such violence that he was utterly confused as to direction. His arms were like lead, he was numb with cold. But with grim tenacity he fought to keep his head above the raging waters, gulping misty air every time his mouth and nose cleared the splashing waves.

On and on; Time had no meaning here in this black void with the roar of the waters dinning back from the low roof and rock walls of the passage. Distance was not measured by feet or yards or even miles; it was an endlessly uncoiling spool of darkness, cold and terrible sound.

The sound was increasing. It was more than the reverberating din flung back from walls and roof by the passing of the waters. It grew to a growing thunder, a shuddering roar.

"A fall!" the Ranger gasped between chattering teeth. "Over that, and I'm done."

Madly he struggled to make headway against the current, to fight in a slantwise direction toward the wall of the tunnel. There might be a strip of beach there, or something to cling to. Further than that he did not plan: it was the instinctive urge to prolong life as much as possible; upon circumstances and conditions depended the next move.

Even the Hawk's great strength was failing under his terrific exertions and the bite of the icy water. A numbness pervaded his body, his brain dulled, his limbs faltered. Only the grim tenacity of his will kept him battling the current.

Slowly, slowly, he won from the center of the stream, where the current was strongest. He was at no great distance from the unseen wall, as the beating-back roar of the echoes told him, when the underground river abruptly changed direction. There was an eddy near the right wall, and into this he was swept. With dizzy speed he spun around and around, still hurtling down stream at the same time. And as he reached the apex of the curve, the thunder of the fall drowned all other sounds. He was on its very brink.

But at that instant his feet touched bottom. The eddy had whirled him shoreward and into shallower water. He struggled, got a purchase on the sloping stone, slipped, floundered, surged forward in a final supreme effort, struggled erect. The water coiled and hissed about his waist. Another step and it had dropped to his thighs, his knees. Gasping, retching, shaking as with ague from cold and fatigue, he stumbled forward and fell face downward on dry ground.

For a long time the Ranger lay prostrate without sound or motion, and not more than half conscious. Gradually his strength came back, his teeth ceased to chatter, his limbs lost some of their numbness. Once out of the icy water, he found the air of the tunnel was fairly warm.

Finally he sat up and made shift to wring some of the water from his sodden clothes. He discarded his soaked chaps and let them lie. His guns were still firmly in their wet holsters and mechanically he drew them and dried them as best he could. They were well oiled and greased and he had little fear of them not being in perfect working condition. The same applied to the greased cartridges in his belt. He emptied his boots of water and drew them on again with considerable difficulty.

Then he stood up, his ears filled with the roar of the nearby fall, his eyes straining to pierce the impenetrable darkness. He had matches in a corked bottle that resisted any drenching. The bottle was unbroken, the matches dry. He managed to strike one on the rock wall.

The tiny flame flickered up, almost blinding his eyes so long accustomed to absolute darkness; but before it winked out, Slade glimpsed a dark opening directly ahead. The straight line of the passage evidently continued after the river veered sharply to plunge over the fall that resulted immediately after it changed direction.

"Well," the Ranger muttered as the darkness closed in once more, "well, I reckon this hole had oughta go somewhere; to the outside mebbe. The air in here is pretty fresh, which would hardly be the case if there was but one outlet. Let's go see."

He groped along the wall and entered the tunnel. As he did so, the noise of the river dimmed. Soon it was a murmur, a dying drone that could no longer pierce the rock wall. Walt Slade was very thankful to leave behind this tumultuous overflow from the pool at the base of the cliff, although to it he undoubtedly owed his life.

The air of the tunnel had a musty, sulphurous tang, but it was not altogether bad. The darkness was so dense it seemed almost to have substance. But there was a grateful warmth in the passage that drove the chill from the Ranger's bones, and his strength quickly returned. He stumbled on through the darkness, treading the dust of centuries and breathing the stale stench of sulphur.

Had there been branches to the passage, he might easily have become hopelessly confused and lost, but the molten lava or expanding gas which, ages before, had doubtless forced its way to the surface by their channel, had found no offshoots of strata as penetrable as the inlay first broken through.

A finger of lurid light was the first indication that he was reaching the end of the passage. The finger rapidly enlarged, was merged with a flooding silvery radiance. Half-blinded, Slade stepped into a strange and weird scene.

It was a roughly circular amphitheater, possibly a quarter mile in diameter, with almost perpendicular walls, ranging from a height of a hundred to maybe twice a hundred feet to the sky-|crowned rim. Beyond the rim and set back at some considerable distance, he could make out towering walls shooting up for seven hundred or a thou-sand feet.

The floor of the vast, well-like cavity in which he stood was formed of cooled lava, honeycombed by fumaroles and hardened bubbles. From some of the fumaroles pulsed a dull glow; it was particularly strong as it poured from a wide opening almost directly in front of the tunnel mouth. Streamers of hot, gaseous vapor, which dissolved and vanished almost immediately upon striking the upper air, arose from the fumaroles and the irregular cracks which frescoed the lava bubbles.

The ground nearby and the rock wall from which the tunnel emerged were splotched and splashed with great gouts of a black, sticky substance that had apparently been belched from the gaping mouth of the crate opening at his feet. Much of it was still warm to the touch, and it dimpled under his fingers in a manner that subtly called something to mind.

Cautiously, holding his breath against the noxious fumes, Slade moved toward the great fumarole and leaned over its crusted edge. From the depths arose the glow which reddened the air about its mouth, and this glow, he could not see, issued from a wide fissure in the dark floor. Into this fissure Slade gazed downward, depth upon vertiginous depth, to where flowed a sluggish stream of a white-hot molten substance, doubtless a still surviving manifestation of the volcano that, untold ages before, had erupted by way of the wide crater in which he stood.

On the floor of the fumarole, which sloped sharply upward to the orifice of the fissure, was further evidence that the infernal fires were not altogether extinguished. The floor was a pool of some dark substance that seethed and hissed with slow, viscous bubblings and with a sound like a huge boiling kettle. It apparently cease-lessly welled up from the unplumbed depths, and with an infinitely slow movement, a slight overflow crept under a low arch which pierced the south wall of the fumarole. Slade stared at the bubbling pool with eyes that suddenly glowed with excitement.

"Asphalt!" he murmured. "Natural liquid asphalt!"

He knew he was right. There could be no doubt about it. Here in one of her mysterious laboratories, Nature was and doubtless had been for uncountable ages, manufacturing with unfathomable patience and slowness of process, the black tar-like substance which splashed the floor and walls of the amphitheatre.

Slade turned his gaze toward these black gouts spread far and wide.

"Musta been plenty of hell hereabouts and not long ago," he mused. "Some kind of an eruption, I reckon—blew the stuff out of the pool and all over the section. Glad I didn't amble out of that gopher burrow right then 'stead of t'night. Nope, it wasn't very far back, either. The stuff hasn't even had time to cool and harden in the open air. That wouldn't take so over long, even though the rocks around here are warm and, I reckon, stay that way."

With glowing eyes he stared at the evidence of recent subterranean violence, and then, with deep satisfaction, gazed down at the bubbling pool. In his heart was exultation, in his mind grim purpose. *He had unriddled the weird secret of the Black Quag!*

Chapter 23

Turning from the fumarole, Walt Slade gazed up at the broken rim of the crater. Overhead, a full moon flooded the sky with silvery light and revealed the scene in every detail. By its radiance Slade saw that on the east side a landslide had formed an approach of detritus at the foot of the slope. Above this the sheer rock had been deeply scarred and chipped by falling boulders. The rim of the crater where the slip had originated was deeply indented, which decreased the height of the wall at that point.

Crossing the crater and wading up the loose talus slope, he began a perilous ascent of the wall. Taking advantage of each hollow and nodule, he progressed slowly but surely. For more than fifty feet he climbed straight up, feeling rather than seeing his way. At length he reached the massive gash where the rim had broken and fallen into the bottom of the crater. Here the going was much easier and soon he panted to the rim.

Moving away from the rim, Slade gazed about him. He was in a canyon, a canyon with steeply sloping walls towering up for hundreds of feet. It was wild and desolate, its floor thickly overgrown with tangled brush and stunted trees.

Only about the blackened rim of the crater was naked rock. To the north were rugged hills, also to the west.

Slade studied the surrounding hills in an endeavor to get his bearing. Suddenly he uttered an exclamation. He recognized, now, the configuration of the hills to the north. He recalled descriptions of the grim canyon which slashed the northern terrain of the XTI range. Yes, this was without a doubt *La Entrada Enfierno*—Hell-Mouth Canyon—and Slade vividly understood now, how the sinister gorge got its unusual name.

He approached the east wall. It was steep and rugged, but not unclimbable, even by the uncertain light of the dying moon. After resting a few minutes he began the ascent. It took him longer than he had anticipated, for after the moon had set he was forced to curl up on a ledge and await the dawn. It was altogether too hazardous to negotiate the uncertain slope in complete darkness. He slept for a while, and awakened stiff and cold, and devoutly thankful for the rosy glow that was creeping up the eastern sky.

It was full daylight when at last he climbed out onto the valley floor and gazed back into the depths he had left behind. Light was flowing into the gorge like water and he could trace the outline of the crater, barely discernible amid the tangle of dark growth.

"Unless a jigger happened to know it was

down there, he wouldn't notice it from up here, the chances are," he told himself.

He turned his back on the canyon and set out down the valley. It was past mid-afternoon when at last, footsore and weary and famished with hunger, he stumbled into the kitchen of the Slash K ranchhouse.

Old Press Thomas, the cook, who had been with Keith Gordon for years, started up with a startled oath as the Ranger entered.

"Good gosh, where'd you come from?" he demanded, staring in amazement at Slade's torn and wrinkled garments and his haggard face.

Slade did not answer, but countered with an abrupt question:

"Where's Gordon?"

"Down to the construction camp," the cook replied. "Ev'body's down there, I reckon—Keith and the other spread owners here in the valley and Thorne, the bank president, and the railroad men."

"Get me something to eat and drink *pronto*," Slade ordered. "What they doing down there?"

"Ain't you heard?" wondered the cook as he busied himself preparing a meal. "They're settlin' this damn railroad bus'ness t'day. Wade Thorne, the banker, has agreed to take over all the spreads in the valley and advance enough money to finish buildin' the railroad through to the mines."

"Gordon's spread, too?" Slade asked quickly. "Gordon can meet his note. He doesn't hafta worry."

The cook shrugged his scrawny shoulders. "Well, you know how Keith is," he replied. "Thorne won't advance the money unless he can control the hull valley. He says that's the only way he can 'spect to get his money back. So Keith is sellin' out to him to save the other boys. Thorne will foreclose on them if he don't, and they'll lose all the money they put inter the dadgummed railroad, too. This way, they won't lose ev'thin'. Darned fine of Keith. I happen to know he hates to let this spread go. It's sorta home to him, I reckon."

Slade was washing up as he listened. Now he turned his gray eyes upon the old cook and they were icier than the water of the underground river which had come so near to claiming him for its victim.

"Put that chuck on the table, and then get the rig on my horse Shadow and bring him to the door," he ordered.

The cook, whose duties did not include those of a wrangler, looked once into those icy eyes, and moved faster than he had done for many a day.

His strength revived by food and drink, Walt Slade swung into the saddle and turned Shadow's head down valley. And at that very moment, a locomotive boomed out of the distant town of Cienaga, headed north over the new line. It pulled a single coach, a long green-and-gold splendor with *Winona* stencilled upon its gleaming sides. And in the coach, tapping his desk top with impatient fingers, sat the blocky, broad-shouldered form of C & P General Manager James G. "Jaggers" Dunn.

The gathering in the construction office had adjourned to the scene of the recent disaster before completing the business at hand. Duncan Taylor still stubbornly advised another attempt at building across the Quag. Keith Gordon just as stubbornly objected, holding out for the Tonto Pass route, and he had unexpected support from Wade Thorne.

Against this united front, Taylor was weakening. He knew that the hope that the whole line would not be abandoned depended upon the local backers raising more money. But, contentious to the last, he had suggested that the gathering come and see the new preparations he had made for a further assault upon the sinister swamp. Standing on the lip of the pool of muck, not yet crusted over, that washed the granitewall at the mouth of the valley, he argued and gesticulated, driving home his points with a stabbing forefinger.

Keith Gordon, resting a hand on the shoulder of his mustached head bartender, old Ben Ward, listened wearily, too courteous and considerate to deny the engineer this last chance to present his case. Nearby stood Wade Thorne, wearing his perpetual half-smile. Beside him was his spread foreman, the beetle-browed Bunch Mawson, and two hard-faced cowboys. Allison, Taylor's assistant, flanked the group, a derisive expression on his floridly handsome face. Lounging a little apart, and evidently bored with the proceedings, was Sheriff Clate Shaw, powerful hands hooked over his gun belt. He glanced idly down the valley, and uttered a sharp exclamation.

A rider was speeding up the valley, fearlessly traversing the treacherous green surface of the Quag. The slanting sunrays gleamed on the coat of his magnificent horse.

"Who in blazes is that blankety-blank loco hombre?" wondered Shaw. "Don't he know any better'n to ride there? He—hell, it's that big jigger, Slade!"

Another moment and the great black horse had foamed up to the group. The tall form of Walt Slade swung to the ground. His face was bleak as if carved from granite, his eyes like polished steel.

But it was neither the face of doom nor the terrible eyes upon which the gaze of the group focused, some in unbelieving amazement. Pinned to his blue shirt was a *silver star,* the honored, feared and respected badge of the Arizona Rangers!

"Good gosh!" gabbled Clate Shaw. "He's a Ranger!"

Old Ben Ward let out a joyous whoop. "I knowed it!" he bawled. "I knowed I had him placed right. Gentlemen, hush! He's a Ranger, all right, and that ain't all. That's the Hawk!"

A hush settled over the tense group. Men stared at the almost legendary figure, Captain Burt Morton's famous lieutenant and ace man, whose exploits were the subject of admiring talk wherever stalwart men of the outlands got together. The Hawk!

Slade paid no attention to Shaw's stutter or Ward's yell. His eyes were fixed on the suddenly tight group across from where Keith Gordon and the engineer stood. His voice rang out, silver-clear, edged with steel.

"In the name of the state of Arizona, I arrest for robbery and murder—Bunch Mawson, Frank Allison, and 'Draw and Fill' Thornton, otherwise known as Wade Thorne!"

For a crawling instant there was stunned silence. Then Bunch Mawson uttered a muffled bellow and went for his gun. Slade shot him, his big Colt clearing leather while Mawson was still reaching. The XTI foreman floundered to the ground, a black hole between his staring eyes. A second shot knocked Frank Allison off his feet, blood pouring from his smashed shoulder.

Slade weaved aside as Wade Thorne drew from his shoulder holster with blinding speed. Slade fired even as the banker pressed trigger. The heavy slug from the Ranger's Colt smashed the lock of Thorne's gun and knocked it spinning. The ex-gambler reeled back, clutching at his bleeding hand, screaming curses. Back and back—a roar of warning—

Too late Thorne realized his danger! He was directly over the yawning mouth of the muck-filled right-of-way. He grabbed frantically at the empty air, tried to regain his balance, and fell backward into the glassy black mud of the Quag. One bubbling, terror-shattered scream, a swirl and gurgle, then the softly lapping waves of ooze rolled over their doomed victim in slow, reptilian coilings and were still.

The two XTI punchers had also "reached", only to freeze in grotesque attitudes under the frowning twin muzzles of the Hawk's guns.

"Get their hardware, Shaw," Slade told the sheriff. "You'll need those two hombres to lead you and yore posse to the Shotgun Riders' hangout. You can bag the rest of the gang t'night without firing a shot."

The wounded Allison had been hauled to his feet and stood glaring and mouthing. All eyes were fixed on him and nobody noticed the stocky, broad-shouldered figure that came hurrying forward from the railroad yards. It was the brittle voice of General Manager Dunn that first awared the group of his arrival. He had halted, and was staring at the cursing Allison.

Allison glared at the executive, his gaze flickered to the Hawk and in his rage his voice took on a thick foreign accent.

"Ach! That Teufel-hundt! From the grave come back! Were it not for him—"

He broke into incoherent ravings that ended in a spasmodic gasping for breath.

Walt Slade gazed at the frantic man, and his gray eyes were sad, his stern face regretful. He shook his head.

"With yore brain, Allison, with yore ability as an engineer, yore knowledge, yore genius! Why couldn't you stay straight and put them to the great use for which they were intended?"

And the tortured lips of Allison, who had been Franz Wolman, honor man of one of earth's most famous universities, seemed to frame in soundless agony, that terrible word—*Why!*

Chapter 24

Later, in the construction office, General Manager Dunn asked a question.

"How did you come to hire that crooked genius?" he demanded of Duncan Taylor.

"Wade Thorne introduced him and recommended him," Taylor explained. "He said Allison was a friend of his, a good surveyor and in need of a job. That was a year ago, when I first came out here to run the original survey. Allison ran the lines up Cienaga Valley. He was always a good worker but never showed any signs of unusual ability or experience."

"He wouldn't," Dunn replied grimly. "He's been run out of half the countries of the world and if he didn't bear a charmed life he would have been killed a dozen times over. The man's a devil."

"Wade Thorne was the moving power back of the whole scheme," Slade said. "He was a crooked Mississippi River gambler and contacted Allison in the old days. They met again after Thorne came out here with forged recommendations from the Dallas bank and set up in business. Allison got a look at this valley, which is an unusual formation from a geologist's point of view. He became interested, explored it, went down into Devil-Mouth Canyon and found the crater there and that welling of natural asphalt. It didn't take long for an engineer of Allison's ability to figure the whole thing out.

"He realized, as I did later, that the asphalt had been forming there for ages and slowly seeping down to this end of Cienaga Valley. He knew that the valley is nothing but a great rock-walled trough, trending to a funnel shape at this end with the slope of the trough toward the north. He figured that there was a great pool of natural asphalt down here under the Black Quag. The asphalt, of course, is chiefly responsible for the Quag.

"Doubtless the belt of stiff clay roofed a natural reservoir of some kind, millions of years ago, or perhaps the whole formation was caused by some vast upheaval, or volcanic eruption. That reservoir was perhaps filled with water, with mebbe a thin roof of stone over it, upon which the clay rested. Perhaps the stone roof fell in and now lies in fragments at the bottom of the reservoir. Then the hot, liquid asphalt began to make its way through subterranean channels into the reservoir. Mebbe the water had drained off. Mebbe the asphalt did fill the reservoir, forcing the clay upward and gradually extending back up the trough.

"Surface water seeped down, the clay became waterlogged, for the water could not penetrate the asphalt. Eroded sand built upon the clay, loam formed upon the sand. Surface water still seeped in and turned the sand and loam into a watery muck which became the Quag. The upper slope of the valley reversed and the overflow of water drained to the nawth by way of subterranean channels. Of course the soft muck of the slough under the thin rind of dried loam and vegetation wouldn't hold any great weight. The clay in turn rested on the yielding surface of the asphalt. When undue weight was placed on any part of the surface, the clay would move and slide, the upper crust would break and whatever was on the surface would be swallowed up and gradually sink on through and into the asphalt. That's what happened to yore railroad, Taylor."

"But what caused that awful noise we heard?" asked Gordon. "It's been heard before, too, according to the stories about the Quag."

Slade chuckled. "That helped the stories to grow, too, I've a notion," he replied. "It 'pears that all hell busts loose up there in the crater where they 'manufacture' the asphalt. I imagine it is erupting steam that blows down through the subterranean passages and bubbles up the asphalt pool. When that happens, it loosens up the whole Quag and anything on it sinks *pronto*."

"Thorne and Allison wanted the asphalt," remarked Jaggers Dunn.

"That's right," Slade agreed. "They realized

that this big pool is worth a fortune. It wouldn't be as big as the world famous lakes on the island of Trinidad, but it's worth plenty. They hadda get hold of the land some way, but the new railroad was going to buy from Gordon. He didn't want to sell, anyway, and if they started offering too big a price he would get suspicious and investigate to find out what made the land valuable. So Allison persuaded Taylor to build over the Quag. He knew the road would never stand and that sooner or later the cattlemen would lose their investment and their land.

"But Gordon was making money and would be able to meet his note at the bank, or so Thorne feared. So he and Allison organized the Shotgun Riders outa hellions they usta hang out with in the old days. That was first-off to raid Thorne's herds and to steal gold shipments from the mine he had a big interest in. Nacherly those hellions got outa hand and committed more crimes. Allison led them."

"He would kill and steal just for the thrill of it," growled Jaggers Dunn. "I tell you, the man's a devil."

"Yeah, they were a salty outfit," Slade agreed. "They had quite an organization, too. Thorne took Clate Shaw inter camp so's he'd allus know what was going on in the sheriff's office. Isn't that right, Clate?"

"Yeah," Shaw admitted, flushing miserably.

"I'd never been 'round any and I ain't eddicated and never had much. I thought it was purty fine to be friends with a banker like Thorne. I reckon I was just a plumb fool."

Slade laid a comforting hand on the sheriff's shoulder.

"You're an honest man, and not afraid to say so when you are wrong," he said, "and that's a lot finer even than being smart and educated."

Shaw gave him a grateful look, and Slade continued:

"Thorne learned, of co'hse, that the framed-up bank robbery had been witnessed and that Allison's face had been seen. That job was just to make things look good for Thorne—his bank being robbed by the Shotgun Riders; but his cashier wasn't in on the deal. He put up a fight and got killed. They hadda get rid of the witness 'fore Sheriff Hank Bevins had a talk with him.

"They slipped up on him at fust and downed Bevins when they thought they were gonna get t'gether. Then they pegged that pore devil out for the vultures, more of Allison's nice notions. But they overlooked that statement in his pocket, and then Bunch Mawson lied to me when I asked him about Crisp Bayles, the man they'd murdered. That was one of my tie-ups. I'd already gotten sorta leery about Allison and Thorne. Thorne was allus around when things happened. Like the night the Sheriff was killed and those bodies were burned up in Doc Groves' office.

"Some of the Shotgun Riders worked on the railroad job and those hellions were two of them. They needed to get rid of their bodies before somebody dropped in from the road job, recognized them and mebbe tied them up with Allison. They'd gotten worried about me and tried to blow me up in the stable. Shadow headed that one off."

"Did you have anything else on Thorne?" asked Taylor.

"The way he carried and handled a gun," Slade replied. "He used a gambler's draw, and that tied up with the yarn Ben Ward told me. I wired the bank, as you'll rec'lect, Gordon, and they wired back they never heard tell of such a jigger; and Thorne had come inter this section carrying rec'mendations s'posed to come from the Drovers' Exchange in Dallas. Then the gold shipment. I'd already about decided that Clate Shaw wasn't the leader of the Shotgun Riders, despite his black eyes and being big and tall, like ev'body who'd got a look at him described the leader of the Riders. You told Thorne about the gold shipment coming through on that particular day, didn't you Clate?"

Shaw nodded.

"And the hellion we killed during the holdup

had black Quag mud stuck in the eyelets of his laced boots, the kinda boots the construction workers wear. That helped tie up with Allison, who I'd already pegged as leader of the Riders. I knew Allison was off-color, 'cause I'd gone through his desk and discovered he was a highly certified engineer and graduate with high honors of a great university, and he was posing as not much more than a surveyor. In his desk, also, was a briquet of asphalt, and it was just the shape of the boring specimens taken from the Quag. I saw those borings, you'll rec'lect, Taylor.

"You remember telling me how Allison accidentally broke yore glasses and you were nearly blinded without them. It was no accident. He didn't want you to get a good look at those borings. They were not bored straight down through the clay, as they should have been, but at a shallow angle that plowed along the surface of the clay. The graining of the clay showed that clearly to a man with good eyes who knew something of the business."

"Why'd they set the fire in the railroad yards?" asked Clate Shaw.

"To cause more expense and delay. They knew the funds of the new line were running low, and every dollar counted. They couldn't tell for shore, you see, just how much the fill across the Quag would cost and how much loss there would be. They weren't missing any bets. Well, I told you what happened yesterday, when I got a look at Allison's face up there in the gorge, and they gave me up for dead, so I reckon you've got the lowdown on everything."

"I never realized asphalt was so valuable," remarked Keith Gordon.

"Used for lots of things," Slade replied. "Paving streets, to make paints, varnishes, prepared roofing, insulation and rubber substitutes. Worth plenty, and liable to be worth a lot more in the future if we should happen to get inter a war that would cut off our supplies of nacherel rubber. Get busy, Keith, and start dredging out. Will make lots of shipping for the new railroad. She goes through, doesn't she, Mr. Dunn."

"It does, by way of the Tonto Pass," the G. M. replied with decision. "But we'll have a spur here to take care of the asphalt shipments," he added.

Slade stood up, stretching his long arms above his black head.

"Gotta be riding," he announced. "Cap. Burt will be wondering what the blankety-blank has become of me. Was headed his way when I stopped off here to do this little chore. *Adios*, and good luck to ev'body. I'll stop at the spread and get the rest of my outfit, Gordon. *Adios*, and good luck to ev'body."

They watched him ride away, tall and straight

upon his black horse, the last rays of the setting sun etching his stern profile in golden light, a look of pleasant anticipation in his green eyes as he thought of the fresh "chores" of difficulty and danger that Captain Morton would have waiting for the Hawk.

Center Point Large Print
600 Brooks Road / PO Box 1
Thorndike, ME 04986-0001 USA

(207) 568-3717

US & Canada:
1 800 929-9108
www.centerpointlargeprint.com